SHERLOCK HOLMES VS. FRANKENSTEIN

An intriguing mystery lures Sherlock Holmes from the comfort of Baker Street in the winter of 1898: the ghastly murder of a gravedigger in the most bizarre of circumstances. Soon Holmes and Watson are travelling to the tiny German village of Darmstadt, to unmask a callous killer with an even more terrifying motive . . . In nearby Schloss Frankenstein, the eponymous family disowns the rumours attached to its infamous ancestor. But the past cannot be erased, and an old evil is growing strong once again — in the unlikeliest of guises . . .

DAVID WHITEHEAD

SHERLOCK HOLMES VS. FRANKENSTEIN

Complete and Unabridged

LINFORD
Leicester

First published in Great Britain

First Linford Edition
published 2016

Based on the screenplay by Gautier Cazenave

The names, characters and incidents as
portrayed in this book are fictional, and any
resemblance to actual events, locales, organiza-
tions, or persons living or dead is purely
coincidental.

A catalogue record for this book is available
from the British Library.

ISBN 978–1–4448–3061–3

Published by
F. A. Thorpe (Publishing)
Anstey, Leicestershire
Set by Words & Graphics Ltd.
Anstey, Leicestershire
Printed and bound in Great Britain by
T. J. International Ltd., Padstow, Cornwall

This book is printed on acid-free paper

*Dedicated to Peter Cushing
(1913–1994),
who played them both.*

1

The Gravedigger's Murder

Waking from a deep and dreamless sleep, Sherlock Holmes stared up at the ceiling of his small Baker Street bedroom and slowly gathered his thoughts. He had spent the past three days working non-stop on a case that had threatened to tax even his great reserves. But with the puzzling affair of the Bedford Square cab finally solved, he had returned home at seven o'clock the previous evening, convinced that he would sleep for a week.

Pausing only to wrinkle his nose at the cold cuts Mrs Hudson had left out for him, he had gone directly to his room. But sleep had eluded him, at least initially. With Watson absent (no doubt on some dalliance or other), he had finally taken from his shelf a random book with which to occupy himself. Eventually his eyelids had grown heavy, and he had slept.

Now, checking his bedside clock, he saw that he had slept for fourteen blissful hours. As he sat up, the book he had been reading when sleep finally claimed him slid off the bed to land with a thump on the carpet. It was C. W. Wolf's *Apis Mellifica, or The Poison of the Honey-Bee as a Therapeutic Agent*, a volume he hadn't perused in years.

With a languorous stretch, he ran his long, chemical-stained fingers through the raven-black hair that swept back from his high forehead. Habit dictated that he attend to his ablutions and face the new day refreshed. But now that he had concluded his present investigation, where was the motivation for so doing? He had always thrived on mental stimulation. During those periods between cases, the world's first consulting detective did not so much live as simply *exist*, until a new challenge arrived on his doorstep. Such barren periods were always interminable . . . and such a period seemed almost inevitable now.

As he retrieved the book and put it on his beside cabinet, he noticed a slip of paper beside the clock. Scanning the characters briefly, he allowed himself a rare smile.

At almost the same instant he heard two sets of footsteps ascending the stairs, followed by the opening and closing of the sitting-room door to which his bedroom adjoined. Then someone — no prize for knowing it was Watson — knocked tentatively at his door.

'Holmes? Holmes, are you awake?'

'I am,' Holmes replied, throwing back the bed sheets. 'I shall be out directly.'

When he stepped outside a few moments later, clad in a long velvet dressing-gown the colour of dried blood, it was to see Mrs Hudson transferring their breakfast plates from tray to table.

'There you go, sir,' she said. 'Bacon, eggs, a nice piece of poached haddock, toast, coffee — oh, and a lovely bit of ham. As lean as a lath, just how you like it.'

Tall and spare, with a thin face, a hatchet-blade of a nose and a square, determined chin, Holmes pointedly crossed instead to the Persian slipper hanging from the mantelpiece. There he proceeded to fill his blackened clay pipe with rough-cut shag.

'You assume that I am hungry, Mrs Hudson,' he said peevishly. 'You should *never* assume.'

Watson — a sturdy, enviably athletic figure with handsome features and a neatly trimmed moustache — had already taken his place at the table. Now he shook his head in exasperation. 'Holmes, you haven't eaten for the better part of three days. If you are not even the slightest bit hungry now, then I fear there is something seriously wrong with you.'

'Dr Watson's right, sir,' said Mrs Hudson in her gentle Scottish brogue. 'You're not as young as you used to be, Mr. Holmes. You *have* to eat.'

'I am two years younger than the good

doctor, here,' Holmes returned with just a hint of petulance, patting his pockets in search of matches. 'Besides which, forty-four is hardly old.'

'But you're older today than you were this time yesterday,' Watson pointed out cheerfully, gesturing to the table in a manner that brooked no argument. 'Now — eat.'

'Doctor's orders?' grumbled Holmes, reluctantly setting the pipe aside.

'If that's what it takes to get you to rebuild your constitution, yes.'

On her way to the door, Mrs Hudson said, 'Be sure to keep a little enthusiasm for dinner, sir. I intend to make spotted dick with candied fruit.'

'I can hardly wait,' Holmes muttered acerbically. But he had to confess, even if only to himself, that the morning's repast did look rather appetizing.

As their landlady bustled from the room, Watson said, 'Given that you have finally succumbed to exhaustion, may I assume that the mystery of the Bedford Square cab has been solved at last?'

'Is that what you intend to call it when

you seek to publish it?'

'*The Adventure of the Bedford Square Cab*, actually. Do you think it will make a good story?'

'Not unless you invent any number of dramatic twists to spice it up.'

'I would hardly consider doing that.'

'Then to answer your question, Watson — no, it would *not* make a good story. In the event, it was little more than a puzzle for the mind.'

'And yet it took you three days to unravel it.'

'Indeed. And it should never have done so, for the answer was plain to see right from the start.'

'The answer being . . . ?'

'A simple calculation,' Holmes replied, slicing into his bacon. 'All that was needed was to work out how quickly the wet tyre tracks of a hansom cab take to evaporate on a cobbled street, given the unseasonably mild conditions of the night in question. Once I had a satisfactory answer to that, the rest was — '

' — elementary?'

Holmes winced. 'An overused word, if

ever there was one, but accurate enough in the circumstances. Now, pass the marmalade, will you?'

As he obliged, Watson asked, 'Did you see my note? The Dancing Men?'

'I did, indeed. 'Breakfast time'. Very clever!'

'Thank you.'

'To what do I owe the honour of all this attention, anyway? Or is it that you simply share Mrs Hudson's concern for my advanced age?'

Watson's good humour faded. 'I only try to keep you busy in mind and body,' he replied softly, 'so that you don't resort to — '

' — my 'drug mania', as you have been pleased to call it in the past?' Holmes finished. 'The 'fiend' within me that is 'not dead but sleeping'?' A smile that was more a twitch than anything else touched his thin lips. 'I almost considered it last night,' he confessed, 'though not to stimulate, but rather to relax. Instead, I turned my attentions to a most fascinating book espousing the homeopathic benefits of beeswax.'

'A much wiser choice,' said Watson, picking up the small stack of envelopes Mrs Hudson had left on the edge of the table. 'Now,' he continued, 'let us see what the day's first post has to offer.'

Halfway through his inspection he paused to study one envelope in particular. 'I say,' he remarked, 'this one looks interesting.'

'The one from Darmstadt, Germany, you mean?' asked Holmes, busily buttering toast. Watson looked at him. 'You have been expecting it?'

'Not at all.'

'Then how — '

'Although I cannot see the face of the envelope, Watson, I can see the back clearly enough — and the return address that all overseas mail requires to be written there.'

Watson sagged, for the answer was so obvious he should have seen it for himself. 'Anything else you would care to share with me?' he enquired, and when Holmes reached for the envelope, he quickly withdrew it with a mischievous, 'Ah-ah-ah.'

Holmes fell into a disapproving silence.

His ability to see the things that were all too often overlooked by others was not a parlour trick designed for amusement. Nevertheless, he said, almost wearily, 'The letter is clearly from a man of some education, with a particular knowledge of the law. He is well-trusted and of good reputation, and approximately sixty years of age. He is reliable, fastidious, and he speaks English.'

Watson could hardly repress a smile. 'And you can tell all of this because . . . ?'

'Though graphology has yet to be accepted as a legitimate science, there is much evidence as to the accuracy of its conclusions. The neatness of our correspondent's penmanship, for example, is a sure sign of his reliability. The fact that he uses chromatic ink of high quality — manufactured by the Huber Company of Munich, unless I am sadly mistaken — when there are almost certainly cheaper, though inferior, brands available to him — shows his fastidiousness. You will note that above the return address he has elected to use the English word *From*, rather than the German word *Absender*.'

'And his age?'

'His handwriting is of a style I recognize as old German script, or German cursive. It dates back to medieval times, but has undergone many changes since its inception. The style in which the return address is written — based upon the use of capital letters and umlauts — would appear to date back to the late 1840s ... for argument's sake, let us round it down to fifty years ago. The writer therefore learned this style when he was approximately ten years of age.

'You may add to this the fact that the wax seal accompanying the return address identifies him as the burgomaster, or mayor, of Darmstadt. Since one of the burgomaster's duties is to act as a chief magistrate in local affairs, we may safely say that he has knowledge of the law. And finally, since the position he occupies is an elected one, he must be a man who inspires trust in others.'

Pausing, he added, 'Of course, even *I* am unable to deduce what the mayor of Darmstadt requires of me until I open the letter.'

Taking the hint, Watson handed it over. Holmes used the butter knife to slit the envelope, then extracted a long, single sheet of foolscap, which he read in silence.

'Anything of interest?' Watson asked after a moment.

Holmes passed the letter across. 'Singularly so,' he replied.

Watson took the letter and read:

Simon Helder,
Burgomaster,
Rathaus,
Darmstadt,
GERMANY
7th November 1898

Dear Mr. Holmes,

I know that the demands upon you must be many and pressing. However, I write now in the hope that you will help me to exculpate and protect one of the oldest, noblest and yet much-maligned names in Germany. I am, of course, familiar with your reputation, so am assured that the events I now lay before you will be treated in the utmost confidence.

The village of Darmstadt is a small hamlet set upon the Upper Rhine Plain, with a population of some three hundred inhabitants. Among its claims to fame is the nearby Technical University, which established the world's first faculty for electrical engineering. But Darmstadt itself has also laboured under a dark shadow for these past eighty years — a shadow that, over the past few days, has grown darker still.

The events about which I now seek your assistance are, briefly, these:

On the late afternoon of the 4th instant, a chilly and somewhat dreary day when sensible folk were at their hearths, a young girl named Maria Richter (the daughter of a local doctor, Lars Richter) was at the Freihof Breuberg, a small and relatively remote cemetery on the southern outskirts of the town. Her purpose there was to gather rhododendrons, since this, curiously, is the only place in Darmstadt where they grow in abundance.

The girl, who is eight, was interrupted from her task by the sound of raised voices. Curious, she was drawn to the sound and from a distance observed the combination gravedigger-caretaker of the cemetery, Mauritz Färber by name, in heated discussion with a man with whom she was not familiar. This man, who was dressed in a long, somewhat ragged black caped coat, had his back to the girl, so all she could supply about him afterwards was an impression of his size, as judged against Färber, who is himself exceptionally tall. The stranger was described as enormous — certainly taller and bulkier than the average man, with longish, unkempt black hair.

The argument in which the two men were involved suddenly boiled over, and the large stranger virtually threw himself at Färber, whose scream chilled young Maria's blood and sent her fleeing from the cemetery, leaving a trail of rhododendrons in her wake.

She went at once to her father, a surgeon of some renown (and director of Saint Corbinian's Hospital), to report what she had witnessed. Convinced by the girl's sincerity that she had clearly seen something greatly distressing, Dr Richter himself returned to the cemetery, but found no trace of either Mauritz Färber or the stranger. There was, however, clear evidence of a struggle at the spot his little Maria had indicated, and a strong smell as of aged whiskey, which implied that the argument had been fuelled by drink.

Dr Richter called at Färber's lodgings, but he was not at home. Nor was he seen for the next two days — until yesterday, when his body was discovered, clumsily hidden beneath rocks beside a wooded stream several kilometres away. His neck had been broken, and his left leg was missing. The leg has yet to be found.

Out of concern for the family to which I alluded in my opening paragraph, our local constable, Oberwachtmeister Reiniger, and I have taken the unusual step of withholding this unfortunate business from the wider authorities, at least temporarily. Herr Färber was a bachelor who lived alone, and though popular among a certain class, is unlikely to be missed to any great extent, at least for a short while. My hope is that, in the interim, you might come to Darmstadt as my guest and solve this dreadful murder with all discretion.

And that Färber was murdered is quite beyond dispute. I am assured by Dr Richter that the bruises discovered upon his throat are consistent with those of strangulation. However, such was the force — perhaps fury? — with which he was attacked, that the cervical vertebrae were quite literally crushed.

As for the leg — and here, Mr Holmes, is the fact I find most disturbing of all — it appears to have been removed post-mortem by someone with clear medical knowledge.

Watson looked up. 'Good grief!' he declared, setting the letter aside. 'What a ghastly affair! But I believe this burgomaster fellow has allowed his imagination to run away with him.'

'Oh?'

'Well, by his own admission the body was found in wooded country after two days. Plenty of time for wild animals to have feasted upon the corpse — '

'And amputated the leg?'

Watson bristled at that, for he was justifiably proud of his profession, and rabidly protective of it. 'He does not say *amputated*, he says *removed*,' he pointed out. 'Now — do you have any idea just how sharp and precise the beak of practically any wild bird can be? As sharp and precise as any scalpel, I assure you. And once loosened, it would be a small matter for . . . I don't know, let us say a hungry bear, maybe even a wild boar, to come along and remove the leg entirely.'

'And yet the burgomaster makes no mention of animal depredation.'

'Then he has overlooked the patently obvious. For what is the alternative? That this mysterious giant killed the gravedigger and made off with his leg? Whatever for?'

'Whatever for, indeed,' Holmes mused softly.

Something in his tone made Watson eye him askance. 'You don't actually intend to take the burgomaster up on his offer, do you? To travel all the way to Germany just to investigate a drunken brawl and an animal attack?'

'That is precisely what I intend to do,' replied Holmes, rising and once again snatching his pipe from the mantelpiece.

'Why?'

'The burgomaster is not so much concerned with catching the murderer as he is with, as he says, 'exculpating and protecting one of the oldest, noblest and yet much-maligned names in Germany.' Can't you guess who he means?'

'I'm sure I cannot.'

'The Frankensteins,' said Holmes.

Watson scowled. 'The Franken — do you mean the book by Mary Shelley?'

'Yes. Although in Mrs Shelley's book, I believe the Frankensteins were described as Swiss . . . doubtless to save the real family any embarrassment. In fact, towards the end of his letter, Herr Helder confirms as much.' He retrieved it and scanned it again. 'Yes — according to him, Schloss Frankenstein, the castle which overlooks Darmstadt, is now owned by Baron Karl von Frankenstein, who would prefer to avoid an official inquiry into the murder so as to spare his family name.'

'Even so . . . I mean, the entire thing sounds like a practical joke to me.'

'Perhaps,' Holmes murmured thoughtfully.

'But you don't think so?'

'I do not.' Finally locating his matches, he puffed the disreputable clay pipe to life, then crossed to one of the room's many bookshelves, where he took down their well-thumbed copy of *Bradshaw's*. 'I shall spend this afternoon at the library and acquaint myself with both Darmstadt and Baron Frankenstein,' he decided, thrusting the bulky railway guide toward Watson as he spoke. 'In the meantime, if you will be so kind as to organize the necessary travel arrangements, I will send a telegram to our friend Helder, and then we can pack for the trip.'

'We?' echoed Watson. 'What makes you think I want any part of this . . . this fool's errand?'

'Because it may well be a monstrously good story for you to write,' Holmes replied with relish. 'Picture, if you will, a bizarre murder, a crazed killer, a suggestion of the occult, and an apparently ageing detective seeking justice and truth in a foreign land. What more could you want?'

'A damsel in distress, perhaps?' Watson suggested hopefully.

Ignoring that, Holmes said, 'In any case . . . '

'What?'

' . . . if you don't come with me, I may have to take my other friend instead.'

Beneath his moustache, Watson's mouth tightened. 'That is blackmail,' he said. 'Furthermore, it is not even remotely amusing, for you well know that I will never rest until you are done with that infernal narcotic once and for all.'

'Then come along, if only to ensure my very best behaviour,' Holmes replied. And without waiting for a response, he went to the door, opened it and called downstairs, 'No spotted dick for us tonight, Mrs Hudson, or we shan't be able to eat strudel the day after tomorrow!'

2

Destination Darmstadt

With little choice in the matter, Watson did as asked and arranged the trip via Cook's in Ludgate Circus. But as their travel itinerary began to take shape, he realized that he was not wholly opposed to the idea of a trip to Germany after all. At the very least, Holmes would find distraction in solving the gravedigger's murder. After that, he, Watson, would do his best to turn their visit into a short holiday from which Holmes's health — and particularly his mental wellbeing, which was fragile even at the best of times — could only benefit.

Thus it was that they caught the nine o'clock train for Dover that same evening, exchanging the frenetic hustle and bustle of London's Charing Cross Station for the relative peace of the suburbs, and thence the Kentish countryside.

Beyond the carriage windows, the night was chilly and damp, and spots of sleety rain dappled and tapped at the glass. Holmes himself passed much of the journey immersed in a book. Once he looked up to ask if Watson had also thought to pack a copy.

'A copy of what?' Watson enquired.

Holmes held the volume up for his friend's inspection. It was Mary Shelley's *Frankenstein, or The Modern Prometheus.*

'Apparently you packed it for me,' came Watson's long-suffering reply. 'That *is* my copy.'

'Another sign of my 'advancing age,' no doubt,' Holmes remarked lightly. 'But I distinctly remember taking you to see the play at the Gaiety Theatre.'

'What a dreadful evening that was!' Watson recalled. 'We stayed up all night discussing how truly awful the performance was.'

'Well, for me it was not so much the performances as the content — or rather, the lack thereof,' Holmes explained. 'It contained so little scientific information.'

'True,' Watson allowed. 'But *Frankenstein*

is a fable, remember, not a biological treatise.'

'If I may coin a phrase, I prefer to call it scientific fiction. A story based on the knowledge of anatomy and medicine at that time.'

'Of course. But even so, it is nonsense — a piece of fluff, nothing more.'

Holmes eyed him thoughtfully before finally saying, 'You surprise me, Watson. I'm amazed that you cannot visualize a world in which life could be manufactured in a laboratory.'

'That is because I'm a doctor, not a wizard. Healing the living has nothing to do with resurrecting the dead.'

'Mary Shelley would seem to agree, since she focused her story more on the melodrama than the question of ethics. But then, she was only eighteen when she wrote it.'

'Indeed. And quite a grim tale for such a young girl, when you think about it.'

'Perhaps. But her life was grim, too, remember. By the age of eighteen she had already experienced several major tragedies. Her mother died a few days after she was born. Her first daughter was born prematurely, and also died within a matter of days. And even after she wrote the book, her life continued to be marred by tragedy. Before she was twenty-five she'd lost three children, a half-sister, an adopted daughter — and, of course, her husband Percy Shelley, who drowned in the Gulf of Spezia.'

It was certainly food for thought. 'Do you suppose it was Mary's fate to go through so much grief?' Watson asked, suddenly thinking of the two wives he had loved and lost, not to mention the wound that had curtailed his career as a military surgeon and left him with a permanent limp.

'Maybe the work itself is part of fate,' Holmes responded.

'That's a bold statement,' said Watson. And not wanting to think about the tragedies that had marked his own life any more than he had to, he took out their copy of *Bradshaw's* and checked their itinerary once more. 'Let's see, now . . . according to the timetable, we should be in Dover by twenty to eleven, and aboard a steamer for Calais shortly thereafter.'

★ ★ ★

They made the connection with plenty of time to spare, and dozed away the choppy sea crossing until the steamer finally docked in Calais at one o'clock in the morning. There followed another uncomfortable four-hour nap until the arrival of the connecting train that would take them through to Darmstadt by way of Brussels, Cologne and finally Frankfurt, where they would make their last connection.

With the rising of a watery sun, the train pulled out of Calais, and the countryside through which they passed quickly became a pleasant patchwork of fields separated by tall hedgerows and ancient forests of oak and beech. Every so often the fields gave way to olive groves, and occasional hamlets that appeared to have changed little since they were first established in the Middle Ages. At those times, Watson sat forward to admire the charm of each such village, with its Flemish architecture and the slow, seemingly unhurried routines of the people who lived there.

As picturesque as the countryside was, however, the five-hundred-mile journey eventually began to pall. In particular, that first day was spent largely in silence, until at last Holmes said, 'When do you propose to tell me what a terrible person I am?'

Watson looked up from the copy of *The Savoy* he had bought in Calais. 'I beg your pardon?'

'You have been decidedly frosty towards me all day,' Holmes replied. 'I was just wondering how long you intend to allow your annoyance to fester before you give it voice.'

'I'm sure I don't know what you mean,' said Watson, knowing exactly what he meant.

'Come, now,' said Holmes, sitting forward with his elbows on his knees. 'You vanish from the waiting room in Calais the minute you think I am asleep; you are gone for a quite inordinate amount of time; and since we boarded the train at dawn you have hardly spoken a handful of civil words to me.'

'It's your imagination,' said Watson,

reaching into his jacket for his pipe and tin of Craven Mixture.

'On the contrary,' said Holmes, 'you left the waiting room in order to examine the contents of my case.'

'How dare you accuse me of such perfidy?'

'Well, someone examined it. As you know, it is of the sturdiest brown leather, manufactured by Messrs Edwards and Sons, with brass locks and thick straps. I rarely trouble myself to lock the case, but I do always make a point of buckling the straps, invariably using the fifth hole in each strap. When I inspected my case this morning, however, one of the straps was only buckled to the fourth hole.'

Watson struck a match. 'That could have been the work of anyone!'

'But it wasn't, was it? Because you obviously found what you were searching for, and have been stewing in your own righteous indignation ever since.'

'Have I, indeed?' countered Watson, his temper slipping. 'And what was I looking for, pray tell?'

'My other friend.'

'I think you are becoming overly mistrustful in that 'old age' you spoke of yesterday.'

'And your attempt at denial, Watson, is as hollow as . . . as . . . '

'A hypodermic needle?' challenged Watson.

And there — it was out in the open at last. Seeing no point in continuing his denial, Watson said, 'Do you remember our agreement, Holmes? That the purpose of my presence on this trip was to keep you on the straight and narrow?'

'And what am I supposed to do when you're not here to provide the stimulation I so clearly require?'

'You could read.'

'My dear friend, I've read everything I possibly can on Darmstadt and the Frankensteins. I can also recite most of Shelley's book by heart.' He stared up at the ceiling of their compartment, as if seeing words there. ''All my past life was now a blot, a blind vacancy in which I distinguished nothing. From my earliest remembrance I had been as I then was in height and proportion. I had never yet seen a being resembling me. What was I? The question again recurred, to be answered only with groans.' Makes you think, do it not?'

'Not just now, thank you all the same,' said Watson, riffling the pages of his magazine as he sought another article to read.

The awkward silence settled between them again, until Holmes suddenly asked, 'Did you bring your service revolver?'

Watson glanced up. 'Of course I did. You specifically requested that I should.'

'I did, indeed. But do you expect to use it while we are in Darmstadt?'

'I sincerely hope not.'

'So you have brought it just in case?'

'I suppose so, yes.'

'Then you should have realized that I have fetched my other friend for much the same reason, Watson. Just in case. And with no real expectation of using it.'

Watson turned a page, not really seeing what he was looking at. 'Very well. I apologize for going through your belongings,' he said at length. 'But I believe you owe me an apology, too — for breaking your word.'

'I never actually *gave* my word — '

'Holmes, I am not in any mood for semantics! Can you not see that I am concerned for you; for the damage you are doing to yourself? You have a brilliant intellect, Holmes, *brilliant*! But for a brilliant man, you can sometimes be as stubborn and stupid as a mule.'

'It is this very intellect you should blame,' Holmes replied, tapping his high forehead with one long index finger. 'For it is a thing every bit as unique as Mary Shelley's creature; something that, for good or ill, is one of a kind. The only other mind that even comes close to mine belongs to my brother . . . and as you know, he and I see each other as little as possible.'

'Even so, you must think of your health, Holmes.'

'That is precisely why I have become a slave to the seven-per-cent solution,' Holmes replied. 'To keep myself from going mad.'

Watson shook his head. 'Then there is nothing to be gained from continuing this conversation. So, if you will excuse me . . . '

'On the contrary,' Holmes responded. 'I have already gained far more from this conversation than you could possibly imagine.'

'Oh?'

Holmes looked directly at Watson and said, 'Think back, if you will, to the line I quoted just moments ago — 'I had never yet seen a being resembling me.' I could say much the same for myself. It is a lonely existence, Watson, and has not always been so through choice. But your concern for my welfare serves to remind me that I will never be truly alone, as long as I have a friend like you.'

Touched by the rare display of appreciation, Watson cleared his throat and returned his attention to his magazine. 'All I ask,' he said without looking up again, 'is that you exercise some caution when using that wretched drug. If Frankenstein's creature doesn't get you first, then I fear your use of cocaine very well might.'

3

Bloody Foreigners

Holmes and Watson were the only passengers to alight when the train finally laboured into Darmstadt's tiny railway station late the following evening. And once it pulled out again barely two minutes later, clanking and chuffing into the wintry darkness, the night grew quiet but for the occasional raucous cry of some questing night bird or other.

Setting down his bags, Watson looked expectantly left, then right, but the station was deserted. No member of staff had come out to greet the train's arrival, just as there had been no sign of any passengers planning to take it on to Heidelberg, where it terminated. He checked his pocket watch. It was a little past ten o'clock.

A lamp was burning dully in what appeared to be a waiting room, but when he tried the door he found it locked. And when he glanced at the flower boxes occupying the windowsills to either side of the door, all that met his gaze were long-dead blooms that now looked brittle to the touch.

'What a wretched-looking place,' he muttered, his words accompanied by a cloud of vapour.

A light, gauzy mist drifted around the lamps that hung unmoving at regular intervals along the platform's gingerbread awning. Beyond the darkened buildings on the opposite platform lay steep forested hills, tar-black with shadow. Toward the southernmost summit, he saw what he took to be a distant square of amber light, as from a window.

Suddenly a great flare of lightning sheared across the sky, and in that brief illumination Watson caught the silhouette of angular, peaked towers and crenelated fieldstone walls rising from among the trees. Then the sky fell dark again, and that venerable edifice — a castle, for surely it could be nothing else — vanished.

'Good grief, Holmes!' he cried. 'Did you see that? Do you suppose it was — '

' — Castle Frankenstein?' finished Holmes, leaning on his cane some distance away. 'Almost certainly.'

Thunder rumbled as if from a faraway battlefield, and Watson shivered. A wind sprang up and the lamps began to sway, causing shadows to stretch and shrink in all directions. 'Do you suppose we are expected?' he said.

'I received a wire confirming as much.'

'Then why is no one here to meet — '

Before he could finish, the station door at the far end of the platform swung open with a screech of dry hinges, and a man's voice called, 'Herr Holmes?'

They turned as the speaker hurried toward them, his black lace-up boots clicking and clacking loudly in the otherwise silent night. As he drew closer, they saw that he was about five feet four inches tall with the slight, wiry build of a jockey. His meagre frame was all but lost beneath a heavy Inverness cloak, and his too-long cotton trousers concertinaed almost comically at his ankles. He was in his mid-twenties, with a pinched, clean-shaven face and smallish features that clustered at its centre. His eyes were bright blue, his fine brown hair an unkempt spill that fell loosely across his forehead.

'Herr Holmes?' he asked again, a little breathlessly. 'Dr Watson? Welcome to Darmstadt. I am sorry I was not here to meet you from the train. I am Franz Liebl, the burgomaster's chief clerk. It will be my great privilege to look after you for the duration of your stay.' The uncertain smile to which he treated them was that of one desperate to please. 'If you will allow me to take your bags . . . ? *Ich danke Ihnen.* Then I will take you to the inn.'

Small though he was, there was obvious strength in Liebl's slight frame. With bags tucked beneath his arms and suitcases held firmly in his smooth but large-knuckled hands, he led them out of the station and onto a small cobbled square bordered by various shops and an especially grand edifice that Watson took to be the Rathaus, or town hall.

Directly before them there stood a modest black-and-red barouche, with a matching pair of chestnut-coloured horses — clearly unhappy about the coming storm — stamping restively in the traces. Paying them no mind, Liebl quickly got the luggage stowed away, and though they didn't need it, insisted upon helping Holmes and Watson into the waiting carriage. Only then did he climb up onto the driver's seat and, with a sharp flick of the reins, get them moving.

In another sizzle of lightning, Watson saw that Darmstadt was every bit as quaint and time-locked as the villages they had passed through during the early stages of their journey. By contrast, however, this town appeared somehow tired and worn down: a jumbled spider web of narrow winding streets that, even allowing for the relative lateness of the hour, seemed curiously devoid of life.

Again there came a rumble of thunder, and they heard the first tentative patter of raindrops on the carriage's collapsible canvas hood. Puddles began to form, and the pavements quickly took on the appearance of patent leather.

Presently the maze of side streets

opened out, and Watson spied lamp-lit windows up ahead. A few moments later Liebl turned the barouche into a small cobbled square right at the very edge of the surrounding forest, and brought it to a stop before an old building of chalet design, complete with exposed beams and decorative eaves that overhung a raised porch. The place was identified by a sign above the door that read, in bold Gothic script,

Das Kleine Gasthaus
Johann Klein, Prop.

Wordlessly, Liebl hopped down and unloaded their baggage, which he carried up to the porch. When he came back, he produced an umbrella from beneath the driver's seat and held it over the two men as they hurried from the carriage to the shelter of the overhang.

'The burgomaster will meet you at the Rathaus at ten in the morning,' Liebl said. 'I will be here to collect you ten minutes before. For now, gentlemen, I bid you goodnight.'

There came another flash of lightning, followed almost immediately by a crash of thunder that seemed to explode directly overhead. Liebl splashed back to the carriage and with a slap of the reins quickly got his team moving again. In short order the barouche turned a corner and was lost to sight. Within seconds, the sound of the team and the rattle of wheels also vanished beneath the persistent hiss of the downpour.

From the nearby forest, a wolf suddenly howled at the moon. It was quickly joined by a whole pack. Watson shivered again and picked up his bags. ''Having a lovely time,'' he said morosely. ''Wish you were here.'' Collecting his own case, Holmes followed him into the hotel.

A bar and drinking area dominated what passed for an open-plan lobby. To reach it they had to skirt between an eclectic jumble of tables and chairs. A big man with a leather apron tied across his pot-belly was methodically drying glasses and stacking them on a shelf behind him. Unless they were much mistaken, this would be the establishment's proprietor, Johann Klein. As Watson closed the door behind them, the man looked up, showing only vague surprise at the appearance of newcomers.

'We're closing,' he said shortly. He was about fifty, with swarthy, pocked skin and prominent blue eyes that may, Watson judged, have been the result of a thyroid deficiency. His thick grey hair was curly and unkempt, the same colour and texture as the goatee that adorned his chin.

'I daresay you are,' replied Holmes, approaching the bar. 'But I believe we are expected. My name is Holmes, and this is my colleague, Dr John Watson.'

Klein nodded slowly. 'Of course. The burgomaster told us you'd be coming.' He turned at the waist, took two keys from a rack and dropped them onto the counter, then brought a register out from a shelf beneath the bar. 'If you'll sign in, I'll have Christina here show you to your rooms.'

Beside the open staircase that led to the upper floors, a young woman with long flaxen hair had been sweeping the floor. She had captured Watson's attention immediately, for she was not unattractive. But her whole demeanour spoke of such sadness and ill use that his heart immediately went out to her — indeed, she seemed sadder than any twenty-year-old should ever be.

'Thank you, Christina — ' he began, doffing his hat.

'Don't try to engage her in conversation,' Klein interrupted gruffly. 'My daughter doesn't talk.'

Holmes glanced at her. 'Doesn't, or can't?'

Ignoring the remark, Klein came around the counter, walking with a noticeable limp. As he cleared the bar, Watson saw that his right leg was missing, and from the knee down he wore a peg of polished teak. Following his gaze, the innkeeper explained brusquely, 'I lost it at Wissembourg in 1870. But I crippled a few Frenchmen, too, before they carried me from the battlefield.'

As Holmes signed the register, Christina brushed past Watson to set her broom aside in the far corner. Instinctively he tried to make eye contact with her, but it was impossible, for she kept her face cast down toward the plank floor. Finally she came back and bent to pick up his luggage, but he wouldn't hear of it. He too bent, but only so that he could put a hand on one slim wrist and stop her. She looked up at him, then quickly looked away again.

'We can carry our own bags, thank you all the same,' he said gently.

Once again her eyes came up to meet his, and he saw that they were large and graphite-grey. She studied his face for a long moment, but her expression showed nothing save bafflement that anyone should ever want to save her from any chore. Beneath her plain ivory-coloured dress, she was tall and thin, possibly even malnourished. Her long, loose-hanging hair framed a heart-shaped face with a tip-tilted nose and full pink lips that were a startling contrast to the pallor of her flawless skin.

Watson said, 'It's — '

Just then the door crashed open,

breaking the moment. A burly man staggered inside, dressed in a heavy pea coat, dirty corduroy trousers and a woollen bowler worn at an angle on his shaggy black hair. Klein, identifying the newcomer, rolled his bulging eyes and shook his head. 'Not you again, Trautmann! I told you, we're closed!'

The burly man only shook his head, spraying raindrops from the brim of his hat. 'You can spare me ten more minutes,' he said, slurring his words in a manner that suggested he had already spent most of his evening imbibing what was no doubt a considerable quantity of Klein's unfiltered wheat beer. 'I mean, iss all right for Nagel and Zeigler. They've got their wives to go home to. But what about me?'

'That's not my concern,' said Klein. 'Now, be off with you. It'll take you a week to sober up as it is.'

Trautmann's lip curled at that. He was an ugly man with a bristly jaw that was both square and pugnacious. His nose was flat, his eyes bloodshot and heavy-lidded, his eyebrows shaggy, the brow ridge itself so low and pronounced that it gave him a perpetual scowl.

'Thass no way to address a customer,' said Trautmann, his voice a low, bubbly growl, and as he said it he threw a lewd wink at Christina that immediately made Watson bristle.

'I think, sir, that you should leave,' said Watson, squaring his shoulders.

Trautmann seemed to notice him for the first time. 'Do you, indeed?' he asked, treating Watson to a myopic scrutiny. 'And you're goin' to make me, are you?'

'No,' said Klein sternly. '*I* will.'

But even as he thumped across the room, Trautmann came to meet him, and with a quick sweep of the foot he knocked Klein's wooden leg out from under him. The innkeeper stumbled and fell hard against one of the tables, which shunted across the floor with a loud, splintery shudder.

Temper spiking, Klein struggled to regain his balance. Before he could do so, however, Holmes set himself between them, facing Trautmann. Trautmann, reading a challenge in Holmes's stance, grinned hugely, and bunching his big fists, came forward in a rush.

Sadly for him, he had no idea that Holmes was a master of *baritsu*, the Japanese system of wrestling. Now, as Holmes went to meet him, he was fully prepared to employ any means necessary to disturb his opponent's equilibrium, to surprise him before he could regain his balance and strength, and to subject the joints of any other part of his body to the strains they were anatomically and mechanically unable to resist. With one swift thrust, Holmes kicked his suitcase across the floor so that it crossed Trautmann's path. Trautmann stumbled forward over it, his already precarious balance immediately lost. Before he could regain it, Holmes upended his cane and hooked the handle around Trautmann's neck and, yanking forward, forced him to the floor. When he was down on the planks Holmes again upended the stick, and this time used the ferrule to pin Trautmann right where he wanted him.

'I would suggest that you yield before any real harm comes to you,' he said.

Down on his stomach and completely disoriented, Trautmann mumbled something unintelligible. He was baffled by the speed with which he had been disabled. Even Watson, who had witnessed Holmes's use of the martial art many times before, was amazed at the smooth precision with which his companion had negated the threat before them.

'Do you yield?' barked Holmes. Trautmann managed to nod. 'Very well. I am placing you upon your honour,' Holmes said sternly, still pinning the man to the floor. 'I expect you to apologize for your behaviour and then leave without further delay.' Trautmann mumbled something and nodded again.

Briskly Holmes withdrew the stick, and then, reaching down, helped the drunk to his feet. Trautmann looked sweaty, flushed and quite thoroughly chastened. 'I 'pologize,' he managed, addressing Klein. But his tone made it clear that the apology had been given grudgingly.

Overlooking that, Klein told him to be on his way. At the door, however, Trautmann couldn't resist having the last word. 'Bloody foreigners,' he sneered, treating Holmes, then Watson, to his fiercest glare. 'You haven't heard the last of me!'

But he quickly lurched back out into the storm before Holmes could treat him to another lesson in *baritsu*.

★   ★   ★

After Christina Klein had shown them to their rooms, Watson took off his overcoat and suit jacket, loosened his tie and flopped onto the bed. The room itself contained only the essentials — a bed, a dresser complete with a bone-china chamber set, a single wardrobe and an armchair.

Another peal of thunder made the casement window rattle, and beads of rain raced each other down the night-black panes. He thought about Castle Frankenstein out there in the stormy night, then about Christina and why she looked so forlorn. What had happened to instil in her such a sense of hopelessness? There was no way to tell yet. But he made up his mind to find out, if at all possible — and then do something about it.

He was still thinking about her when he finally drifted off to sleep half an hour later.

4

The Darkness Before the Light

'Mr. Holmes,' said the burgomaster in a tone well used to making speeches, 'on behalf of the people of Darmstadt, I thank you for answering our call so swiftly. To say that we are honoured to have the most famous detective in the world here in our fair town is an understatement. I simply — '

'You could, perhaps, also take a moment to thank my colleague, Dr Watson,' suggested Holmes, who had little patience for men to whom words came too easily. 'He not only made exactly the same trip as I, but also arranged it for us.'

Though derailed by the interruption, Simon Helder was quick to recover. Of average height and slim build, he was a refined-looking man of about sixty — just as Holmes had deduced from his handwriting — with penetrating brown eyes behind small wire-framed spectacles, and features that seemed somehow to take the very best of male and female and blend them together to form a unique, and not unpleasant, whole. He wore his still-fair hair to the small stiff-pointed collar of his white cotton shirt, at the throat of which he favoured a silk ascot tie of the richest burgundy. The rest of his clothing was of equally good quality, and cut in the latest style — the lapels of his pale grey jacket narrow, the sleeves short enough to show off the cuffs of the shirt.

Now Helder glanced across a desk that was fastidiously tidy but for the presence of several small clockwork toys and other similar items of childish automata — a fisherman with dangling line, a walking, fully clothed jackass, a clockwork elephant — and inclined his head in Watson's direction. 'Quite so, quite so,' he said, his English very good, and with little trace of an accent. 'The inn, gentlemen? I trust it is to your satisfaction?'

'It is perfectly agreeable,' Holmes confirmed irritably. 'But now, if you will, Herr Burgomaster, please tell us about the unfortunate gravedigger.'

The burgomaster sat back, clasped his manicured hands across his bed-of-flowers waistcoat and pursed his lips. The window behind him showed them a dull, chilly morning and scudding clouds that threatened yet more rain.

'There's not really much to say,' he replied. 'Mauritz Färber had worked at the cemetery for as long as I can remember. He saw to his duties in a reasonably dedicated manner and never gave us any cause for complaint.'

'Was he married?'

'No.'

'Friends?'

Helder shrugged dismissively.

'What is that supposed to mean?'

'Fair-weather friends, certainly,' allowed Helder.

'Oh?'

The burgomaster sat forward. 'You must understand something, Herr Holmes. Germany is a modern country and Darmstadt has ambitions to become a modern town. But not everyone has embraced these enlightened times. Old beliefs, old superstitions, old fears . . . they die hard here.'

'Meaning . . . ?'

'Meaning that a man who works — worked — with the dead, who worked among the dead and was perfectly at home doing so . . . is unlikely to be the most popular member of any community. Of course, that is what you might call an occupational hazard. The digging of graves is by its very nature a solitary profession, and few people are comfortable with a friend who earns his living from such a chore. Rightly or wrongly, they still consider it bad luck.

'But when Färber was buying the drinks . . . well, that was a different story. Everyone was his friend then. In any case, Herr Holmes — and I will be perfectly honest with you — the gravedigger's death is of less concern to me than the rumour and gossip that may rise again because of it.'

'Of course. That is why you took it upon yourself to pervert the course of justice, is it not?'

Helder scowled. 'I did not take that decision lightly, Herr Holmes. Indeed, I may yet have to face the consequences. Still . . . '

He opened a drawer and took out a book, which he set down upon the desk. Unsurprisingly, it was a well-thumbed edition of Mary Shelley's novel.

'The Frankenstein family has been burdened with the most unenviable reputation since the beginning of the century,' he said. 'I do not mean to blame Mrs Shelley for that. She could never have foreseen the notoriety her nasty little tale would achieve. But the damage is done. And over the years we have attempted to limit it wherever possible, out of respect for a family who has in my opinion suffered enough.

'Then comes this ghoulish crime. A murderous giant; a missing limb, apparently removed with surgical precision . . . Gentlemen, you can see how such events could be construed — or rather, misconstrued. For that reason, I do not think I overstate the case when I say that the reputation of Baron Karl and his family is at stake.' He put the book back in the drawer.

'Besides the baron, who else lives at the castle?' asked Holmes.

'He has two sons. Clemens is the older boy, though not much of a would-be baron, in my opinion. He's more on the . . . artistic side. And then there's Georg, who is recently back from Vienna, where he has been studying politics. He's the *real* Frankenstein, if you ask me.'

'And the baron's wife?'

'Sadly, she died fifteen years ago.'

'He never remarried?'

'No.'

'Then aside from the usual servants, no one else inhabits Castle Frankenstein?'

'There is Caroline Hertz,' said Helder.

'Go on.'

'The baron was very close to Caroline's father, Dr Rudolph Hertz. They had been friends since adolescence. When Dr Hertz died four years ago, the Frankensteins welcomed Caroline — then left all alone in the world — into their home. A lovely girl, she had always been friends with the two boys, and is now something of a surrogate sister to them.'

'Talking of doctors and daughters,' said

Holmes, 'I should like to have a few words with Dr Richter and his little Maria.'

'You will find the doctor at Saint Corbinian's Hospital,' the burgomaster replied readily. 'Just ask Liebl; he'll take you straight there.'

'Thank you.'

As they rose, Watson took the opportunity to break his long silence. 'You asked about our accommodations, Herr Burgomaster.'

'I did, indeed. I trust that everything — '

'Everything is fine,' said Watson, ignoring the curious look he received from Holmes. 'But . . . it seems an odd coincidence that our host, Herr Klein, lost a leg, just as did Färber.'

Helder frowned. 'Not really. He lost it fighting for the Prussian army, I believe.'

'So he explained. And his daughter . . . '

Holmes's expression changed then, and it said, *I see — Christina has become the damsel in distress you requested back in Baker Street.*

'Christina?' said Helder. 'What about her?'

'As a doctor, I am curious,' Watson explained. 'Was she mute from birth, do you know, or did she suffer some past trauma?'

'Christina hasn't spoken since her mother ran off with a scoundrel some fifteen years ago,' was Helder's reply as he came round his desk to show them to the door. 'The poor child was still quite young.'

'A sad story,' said Watson. 'But such a reaction is all too common. Has she sought medical attention for the condition, do you know?'

'I wouldn't think so,' Helder replied. 'I don't think Herr Klein would allow it.'

'Why not?'

An uncomfortable smile touched the burgomaster's lips. 'A woman who cannot speak,' he explained simply, 'cannot complain.'

★ ★ ★

Saint Corbinian's Hospital was nowhere near as impressive as it sounded. Set in the oldest, poorest section of town, it had long since fallen into decline. Once it had been a clean, bright centre of medical excellence: now it was a tired, dusty shell of its former self, its flaking white-tiled walls and dingy vaulted ceilings echoing with the cries of the diseased and the demented.

A nurse was just crossing the crowded lobby when they entered. Holmes quickly intercepted her and asked her where they might find Dr Richter. Before she could reply, however, an old man staggered up to Holmes and grabbed him by one arm. Toothless, in need of a shave and with his sparse hair awry, the fellow's ragged dressing-gown identified him as a patient.

'*Helft mir!*' he begged pitifully. '*Bitte helft mir!*'

The nurse clucked disapprovingly, and taking the old man by one thin arm, none too gently dragged him away. 'Come along, now, Herr Brunner,' she said sternly, 'back to bed with you!'

'*Nein!*' cried the old man, his voice cracking. '*Oh, mein Gott, nein!*'

As they watched her return him to the ward from which he had evidently just escaped, Watson shook his head. 'The poor devil,' he muttered.

'Indeed.'

'May I help you gentlemen?'

They turned as a tall woman whose soft white hair was pinned up in a bun at the back of her head approached them. Slender and efficient in a pinstripe blouse and dark ankle-length walking skirt, she had bright, intelligent hazel eyes above high cheekbones and a small, pointed chin. 'I am Frau Vogler,' she announced, 'the hospital's almoner.'

'We were hoping to speak to Dr Richter,' Holmes told her.

'And you are . . . ?' she asked, looking from one of them to the other.

'My name is Sherlock H — '

'I *knew* it!' she cried with a sudden, broad smile. 'And you, sir, must be Dr Watson?'

Watson inclined his head. 'Yes, indeed.'

'Gentlemen, what a privilege it is to meet you!' said Frau Vogler, shaking each of them by the hand. 'Before I undertook my present position, I used to be a reader here at Saint Corbinian's. Your stories, Dr

Watson, were always so avidly received by the patients.'

Watson smiled. 'I trust they lost nothing in the translation, Frau Vogler.'

'Not at all,' she assured him.

'Now,' said Holmes, 'about Dr Richter . . . ?'

The almoner returned her attention to him. 'Such a nice man,' she said, 'though being a foreigner — he came to us from Sweden, you see — I fear he has had to work hard to be accepted.'

'May we see him?'

'I am afraid not,' was her response. 'The doctor has been absent for the past two days.'

'Has he, indeed? Do you know where he has gone?'

'I daresay someone does, but unfortunately I don't. I assume he is away on business, or perhaps he has taken leave. He has certainly been working very hard recently, and of course there have been the thefts he has had to deal with as well.'

'Thefts?'

'That is why you are here, isn't it?' she asked. 'Although I would hardly consider them important enough to warrant the attentions of the Great Detective himself.'

'Tell me about them,' said Holmes, deftly avoiding a direct answer to her question.

'I'll happily tell you as much as I know,' agreed Frau Vogler, 'but sadly it isn't much. We have a combination laboratory and pharmacy on the premises, which has recently been subjected to a number of burglaries.'

'What was taken?' Holmes asked keenly.

'That I really couldn't say,' said Frau Vogler, shaking her head. 'As almoner, my concerns are more to do with the patients. But . . . equipment, certainly. Yes. Bell jars, distilling apparatus, at least one . . . knife switch, is it called? . . . that I know about. And, of course, chemicals.'

'Indeed?'

'Oh, yes.' She looked off into the distance, trying to remember details of the thefts. 'Strontium was one,' she said after a moment, pronouncing the word hesitantly. 'Yes. Strontium . . . ammonium vandate, I believe it was called . . . phosphorus . . . iodine. Things of that nature.'

'And the Technical University?' he asked. 'Have they, too, had any recent thefts that you know of?'

'I really couldn't say,' was her reply. 'I daresay I could find out for you.'

'If you would,' he said, 'I should be most grateful.'

Thanking her for her help, they took their leave and descended the stone steps to the waiting barouche. As they climbed into the carriage, Liebl turned and looked at them expectantly.

Holmes said, 'Castle Frankenstein, if you will.'

The burgomaster's clerk, bundled against the damp weather in his overlarge cloak, showed surprise. 'Are you sure, Herr Holmes?'

'Of course. Why?'

'It is a difficult journey, even in good weather,' replied Liebl.

'Nevertheless, that is our destination.'

'Is the baron expecting you?'

'No.'

'I ask because he may not see you without an appointment.'

'He will see *me*, Liebl. Now, if you please . . . ?'

With a snap of his whip, Liebl set the barouche into motion, and the streets, with their occasional horse troughs and tiny shops leaning crookedly against each other, soon yielded to a narrow rutted lane that climbed ever higher through serried ranks of maple and sycamore.

After a time, Holmes muttered, 'Iodine I can understand. It governs thyroid function, I believe?'

Taking his eyes off the scenery, Watson nodded. 'Well, yes. In fact, I believe it could be beneficial in controlling what I suspect to be Herr Klein's thyroid deficiency problem.'

'And phosphorus?'

'It is used in the manufacture of matches, of course,' Watson replied. 'It is also a very useful fertilizer.'

'Its biological role, I mean.'

Watson considered. 'It is essential for the growth and repair of the body's cells, and — Holmes, just what are you getting at here?'

'And strontium?' asked Holmes. 'Ammonium vandate?'

'They promote — ' Watson fell silent.

'I'm waiting,' said Holmes.

Almost grudgingly, Watson said, 'They promote bone growth. But you're not suggesting — '

'I am not suggesting anything,' Holmes replied. 'Yet. But suddenly I have the strongest conviction that this business will get much darker before we are able to shine the light of truth upon exactly what has been happening here in Darmstadt.'

5

Castle Frankenstein

The journey to Castle Frankenstein proved to be as arduous as Liebl had forewarned, and though the rain failed to materialise, the clouds remained heavy and soon took on the colour of lead. As the barouche negotiated one steep switchback after another, a cold wind picked up and scuttled through the heavily forested slopes to either side of the rutted road, making autumn-bare branches rattle and sway. To pass the time, Watson took out his guidebook and, a few moments later, announced that they were travelling on what the Romans had called the *strata montana*.

'The mountain road,' Holmes translated.

'More accurately,' said Watson, 'a road that saddles the mountain. Apparently in Roman times it joined the forts at Limes to the north, and Ladenburg to the — '

A loud crack of sound interrupted him. At first he thought it was the snap of a top-heavy bough finally yielding to the constant tug of the wind. But at almost the same moment a small, splintery hole punched through the door on Holmes's side of the carriage.

'What the — ?' he began. Then: 'Good grief, we're being shot at!'

Even as he spoke, there came another crack — it was easy now to recognize that booming report for exactly what it was — and up on his high seat Liebl clutched at himself, then tumbled sideways to fall from the carriage with a horrified scream.

Unnerved as much by the scream as by the shooting, the horses immediately began to run faster. The reins, now flying loose, whipped and snapped through the air like angry snakes, only encouraging the team to even greater speed.

Snatching out his Webley Mk II, Watson leaned sideways and looked back just in time to see the little clerk roll to a halt in the middle of the road. Whether he was dead or wounded, there was no way to tell.

Holmes, meanwhile, sprang forward and began to drag himself up and over the driver's seat. The barouche, he knew, had no brake — and even if it had, to try using it at such speed would only succeed in turning them over and making a bad situation worse. If he were to avert disaster altogether, he would have to reclaim the reins and bring the horses to a gradual stop.

The barouche careened wildly from side to side, threatening to tip into one of the ditches that bordered the road. For one awful moment Holmes almost lost his grip. Then, hanging on tighter than ever, he finished scrambling over the back of the seat and, leaning forward above the footboard, tried to grab the reins.

The barouche slewed again, and Holmes almost slid right off the board and straight under the spinning front wheels. Facing front again, Watson cried, 'Holmes!' Then the carriage straightened back out, Holmes regained his equilibrium and, undaunted, made another desperate snatch at the reins.

Watson, meanwhile, staggered forward

and, shoving his service revolver back into his pocket, took hold of the back of the driver's seat. He then grabbed a handful of Holmes's overcoat to steady him. Thus braced, Holmes sprang forward, again made a grab at the reins, missed and then tried once more. Around them the woods flashed by in a wild kaleidoscopic blur.

This time he managed to snag one of the long leather lines and wasted no time in furling it around his fist. At the same moment the other snapped towards him and almost took out his eye. Instinctively he flinched back, and when he opened his eyes again the line had temporarily flopped across the lathered rump of the nearside horse.

With Watson still supporting him from behind, he threw caution to the wind and pounced forward, the fingers of his free hand questing desperately for the remaining rein. They found it just as it threatened to slide off the horse's rump and start whipping through the air again. He fumbled it; caught it. Then, with his legs braced against the footboard, he hauled backwards.

'Whoa, there!' he cried. 'Whoa, I say!'

Nothing happened.

'Whoa!'

Still nothing.

'Whoa, there!'

And then, almost imperceptibly, the barouche began to slow.

What seemed like an eternity later, it came to a complete halt in the middle of the high forest road, the horses quivering nervously after their wild run, and Holmes and Watson in a state that was not much better.

* * *

The best part of a mile back down the mountain, Liebl opened his eyes and wondered if he was still alive. He knew that something had struck him in the left arm and pushed him sideways off the coach, but he had no idea what. He did know that it hurt to move his shoulder, however, and that he had obviously winded himself in the fall and passed out, albeit briefly.

Carefully, he rolled onto his side and

sat up. He checked himself over as best he could and satisfied himself that he hadn't broken anything.

So what had happened? And where was the barouche?

Staggering to his feet, he suddenly remembered Herr Holmes and Dr Watson, and groaned miserably. The burgomaster had instructed him to look after them, and he had taken the responsibility to heart. But now there was no sign of the carriage or its occupants.

He started hobbling slowly along the road in pursuit of the carriage, but after a few yards he had to stop, for he was still winded, and every step brought a fresh wave of pain to his shoulder. Again he tried to recollect exactly why he had fallen from the barouche. There had been a sound like a rifle shot, he thought . . . Actually, two such sounds.

He froze. Shots? With a sudden jolt of panic he thought, *Have I been shot?*

Quickly he inspected himself again; and as he did so, something fell from the folds of his overlarge cape to land with a metallic tinkle at his feet. He bent and retrieved it. It was a long, tapered cartridge, now somewhat deformed.

Liebl felt lightheaded. He *had* been shot, then, but somehow the full impact of the bullet had been absorbed by the many folds of the cape.

Nervously he looked around, for the shooter might still be out there somewhere, taking aim at him even now. But the forest on both sides of the road seemed empty, and the only movement came from the cold breeze as it stirred wildflowers and skeletal branches, and carried with it the incongruously cheerful songs of egret and hawfinch.

But who had shot at them, and why? Perhaps it had been nothing more than a careless hunter. He wished he could believe that. But there was evil afoot in this region just now. Look at what had happened to poor Mauritz Färber.

Liebl limped across to an old deadfall and sat down. He would gather his energy and then set off to discover what had become of the carriage and the two *Engländers*. If anything had happened to them, he was finished. He would lose his job, and there could be little hope of ever finding another, for who would ever employ the man — the *fool* — who had unwittingly presided over the injury, or worse, of the great Sherlock Holmes?

The wind died away, and a few moments later a pall of blue-grey fog began to drift down from the mountains. Liebl huddled in his cape and shivered, feeling thoroughly miserable now; far more miserable than a man who had just cheated death had any right to feel.

Suddenly he was startled out of his thoughts by a crunching sound from behind. He twisted, wincing as the movement woke fresh pain in his bruised muscles, and stared into the forest. It was dark as pitch in there, and the trees grew so close together that it was almost impossible to spot what had caused the sound.

Sound . . . That word made him realize that the birdsong had ceased; that the woods had fallen silent but for — and there it was again, the crunching noise, over and over. What in God's name was it?

Then he had it. It was footsteps.

Coming slowly, ponderously closer.

A tingle washed across his skin. Was it the person who had shot him, come to check the results of his handiwork, or to finish the job once and for all?

Instinctively, Liebl slid down off the deadfall so that he was hiding behind it. Crouching as low as he could, head cocked to one side, bright blue eyes growing larger by the moment, he strained his ears.

For several seconds there was only silence. Then the crunching again, getting louder. And something else — a swishing sound, as of great low-hanging branches being brushed aside by someone — some-*thing* — of enormous strength.

Liebl's lips quivered. *He's coming out onto the road*, he thought. *Whoever he is, he's coming out of the forest onto the road, and as soon as he sees me he'll finish me off for good.*

He frowned at a sudden distraction. What was that smell? It reminded him of campfires; of dirt that had been scorched or burned. It reminded him a little of whiskey.

As the source of the sound continued its inexorable approach, Liebl tried to curl into the smallest possible ball he could manage; for the newcomer, this newcomer who sounded so massive, whose very presence had caused the birds to stop singing, had just stepped out onto the road, no more than a few yards away.

An even more complete silence settled over the high mountains. The stink of what Leibl took to be whiskey seemed to block his nostrils. *He's seen me*, he thought. *Of* course *he's seen me! And now —*

But then there came another sound — horses, coming back down the road at speed, a rattle and jingle he recognized immediately as emanating from the barouche.

Please let them get here in time to save me. Not that he had any idea who — or what — he needed to be saved from.

As the sound of the barouche grew louder, the footsteps of whoever had come out of the forest paused. A moment later they picked up again, but this time they were retreating; going slowly, surely, back into the trees.

Liebl thought he was going to pass out with relief. The mist around him began to swirl faster and faster — then, fairly bursting out of it, came the barouche, with Holmes at the reins. Watson, standing at his shoulder immediately behind the driver's seat, stabbed a finger towards the deadfall and cried, 'There he is!'

Holmes brought the carriage to a halt, and the next thing Liebl knew, the two *Engländer* were beside him, helping him gently back up onto the deadfall, and Watson was examining him for injuries.

'Hold still,' said the doctor as Liebl tried to turn toward the forest, from whence his unseen visitor had come. 'Good grief, man, we thought for a moment that — ' He broke off, then finished, 'Never mind what we thought. How do you feel?'

Liebl nodded. 'I am . . . f-fine.'

'Any broken bones?'

'No, Herr Doctor. But — '

'Hold still and let me make sure. That was a nasty fall you took.'

'I am f-fine, *meine Herren*. But I was

71

shot at!' And the little German held up the misshapen cartridge to prove it.

Holmes snatched the bullet from his hand and, holding it in one palm, inspected it minutely through the lens of his pocket magnifying glass.

Now that he was satisfied that Liebl hadn't been seriously injured, Watson fished his Webley back out and began to keep a suspicious watch on their surroundings. 'What does it tell you, Holmes?' he asked.

'The bullet has been damaged by impact, of course, but not as much as it would have had it penetrated our young friend here,' answered Holmes. 'From its size and shape I believe it to have been a round of . . . yes, 6.5 mm. From the scratches on the base of the casing, I suspect that it was hand-loaded by someone not entirely familiar with the true concept of professional factory loading. The insufficient load, coupled with this particular bullet's tendency towards instability when fired, robbed it of its true killing power. The fact that it tumbled end over end instead of flying in a straight line, and thus struck you on its edge, as opposed to its tip, was also instrumental in saving your life, Liebl.'

'And the weapon itself, Holmes?' pressed Watson.

'The calibre suggests only one weapon to me,' Holmes replied. 'I would put my money on a Mannlicher-Carcano carbine.'

'So the bullet tells us everything except why it was fired at us to begin with.'

'As you say. But we know it could not have been accidental. One shot, maybe. Two shots? I think not. We were certainly the targets. As for the why of it, only time will tell us that.'

Holmes put the glass and bullet into his pocket, then placed one gloved hand on Liebl's shoulder. 'Do you feel able to go on, Franz, or would you prefer to go back to Darmstadt?'

'I . . . I am happy to go on,' said Liebl, although in truth he was anything but.

In the event, however, the remainder of the journey passed without further event, although Watson declined to put his service revolver away until the castle finally came into sight through the damp, drifting mist twenty minutes later.

As he looked up at the place, he could hardly suppress a grimace. Built in the thirteenth century, and expanded and fortified in the centuries that followed, Schloss Frankenstein now perched at the very summit of the road. Tall, angular towers studded with tiny windows stood sentinel at the corner of each rough fieldstone 'curtain' wall. As they passed through the open arched gateway into the courtyard beyond, he saw that the castle was actually of quadrangular design, built specifically to protect and defend the range of buildings it housed — a great house, stables, what appeared to be a chapel, and a row of servants' quarters. A more foreboding edifice he had not seen since his first visit to Baskerville Hall, in October of '89.

Liebl turned the barouche and brought it to a halt before the steps leading up to the castle. Disturbed mist spiralled around them. Alerted by their arrival, the door opened and a middle-aged, unsmiling manservant dressed in sober black appeared, eyeing them curiously. Holmes stepped down, and in a tone that brooked no refusal, introduced himself and requested an audience with Baron Frankenstein.

The manservant   bald but for oiled black hair that grew thick above his ears, his olive skin pocked, his nose large and broad, the disapproving slash of his mouth surrounded by a thick beard that was just turning grey — hesitated, them invited them inside and asked them to wait.

The lobby was enormous, with a high vaulted ceiling. Cluttered with heavy furniture, tapestries, and an ornate old Weaver Pump pipe organ, it even boasted a life-size carving of Christ on the cross that was, to Watson's mind, quite appallingly ugly. Portraits of the Frankenstein forebears hung on the gloomy wall beside the wide oak staircase, and antique suits of armour flanked every doorway.

In short order there came the brisk clatter of echoes as the manservant returned to show them into a large, comfortable day room dominated by a massive arched fireplace and a scattering of heavily uphol-stered armchairs and sofas. A piano sat in one corner, a harp in another. The floor was covered in expensive rugs of Peking and Persian design.

A few moments later the door opened again and a heavy-set, imposing man with carelessly brushed white hair and steely pale blue eyes stepped inside. For a moment he merely studied the newcomers. Then he said quietly, 'Good afternoon, gentlemen. I am Baron Frankenstein.'

6

The Bark and the Bite

The hand he offered Holmes had never known hard physical toil. 'Herr Holmes,' he said formally, speaking with hardly any inflection. 'Your name is a most famous one.'

'As indeed is yours, Baron.'

That knowledge only seemed to depress him. He looked every inch a nobleman — distinguished, authoritative, his movements slow and assured, his ruddy face somewhat jowly but nonetheless well-defined, his blue eyes as sharp and incisive as Holmes's own. He wore a black suit with an immaculately tailored frock coat, a white shirt, and a black tie.

'How may I help you, gentlemen?' he enquired. 'If you're investigating the recent murder in Darmstadt, I fear you've wasted your time coming here.'

'Nevertheless,' said Holmes, 'when a

crime is so ghastly, one cannot afford to leave any stone unturned. And though I assure you, Baron, that we have no wish to cause you undue distress, I would like to ask you a few questions.'

'Very well,' he said. The baron crossed the room to the mantelpiece, where he took down a humidor and offered cigars, which they declined.

'You are familiar, of course, with Mary Shelley's book . . . ?' Holmes asked him.

'I am aware of it,' Frankenstein said with no small understatement. 'As I understand it, Mrs Shelley travelled through Germany before she wrote it. She made a stop in Darmstadt, and borrowed my family name with no thought for the consequences. As for the story itself, if such it can be called, she appears to have stolen most of it from her own father's novel, *St. Leon* — the story of a scientist who discovers the elixir of life. Indeed, Mrs Shelley had the audacity to reproduce some of her father's pages almost word for word.'

'Then you are happy to assure us that there is no link whatever between your lineage and the protagonists of that novel?'

The baron hesitated briefly, then offered a resigned sigh. 'I am well aware of your reputation, Herr Holmes, so I will not waste my time or yours by concealing something that you will eventually discover by yourself, anyway. But I must have your word that you will tell no one what I'm about to reveal. Not in England, not in Darmstadt, not even between the walls of this castle.'

'You may rest assured that we are souls of discretion,' said Holmes.

The baron held back a moment longer, then said, 'Victor von Frankenstein did live here, a hundred years ago. His father, Alphonse, was the baron then. In fact, the biographical elements in that woman's book are, for the most part, surprisingly accurate. But there are three exceptions. Setting the story in Switzerland . . . Captain Walton's expedition to the North Pole . . . and, as hardly needs to be said, the existence of the creature. There was no creature. How could there have been?

'You want the truth, gentlemen? Very

well. The truth is that Victor was a failure not only as a man but also as a scientist. Oh, he had a brilliant mind, but all his life he suffered from melancholia — what we now call depression, and several times he was admitted to an asylum, as much for his own safety as anything else. His fiancée, Elizabeth, also suffered immensely from it. She was over eight months pregnant when they married in 1797, but the day after the wedding she and her baby both died.'

'So it wasn't the creature that killed her,' said Watson. 'It was childbirth.'

'It was the absence and the negligence of her husband, Herr Doctor.'

'With respect, I don't see how you can blame it on Victor, Baron. Childbirth is a strictly medical matter. And though there is still a long way to go, the medical profession has made great strides in reducing the number of deaths in childbirth over the last century.'

'Be that as it may,' the baron said with an indifferent gesture, 'the deaths of Elizabeth and her child created a violent reaction within my family. Later that same year, Victor's father, Alphonse, died from shock. Victor himself had a relapse and was once again confined to an asylum. After his release, he cut himself off from the rest of his line and went to live in the Arctic, where he eventually died.'

'As he did in the story.'

'Then you are saying you are not a direct descendant of Victor?' prodded Holmes.

'That is precisely what I am saying! Victor and his brothers all died at an early age and had no heirs, so my grandfather inherited the title of baron.'

'And acted as if Victor never existed.'

The baron eyed him wonderingly. 'Is that really the crime you make it sound like, Herr Holmes? When Shelley's book was published, it sold in vast numbers all over Europe, and it vilified our family name. So we did everything we could to conceal that branch of our family in an attempt to minimise the damage.'

Another uncomfortable silence draped itself across the room. Again Watson felt compelled to break it. 'Baron, we take no pleasure in — '

Before he could finish, the door flew

open and a young man in his early twenties came inside. 'Father! I — ' He froze when he realized that the baron had visitors. 'Oh, I'm s-sorry. Forgive — '

The baron spoke over him. 'Sherlock Holmes, Dr John Watson, may I introduce my son, Clemens. Clemens, these gentlemen have come to investigate that business in Darmstadt.'

Clemens von Frankenstein clicked his heels and shook hands with each of them in turn. Beneath his thick, curly blond hair he had fine pale skin and sensitive features, with well-spaced blue eyes that held rather more compassion than those of his father. His nose was straight, his mouth soft and almost feminine. There was a bloodstained bandage around his left hand.

'I am pleased to meet you, gentlemen,' he said. Then, turning back to his father: 'You have *got* to get rid of that animal!'

With a pained expression, and doubtless feeling the need to explain things, the baron said, 'I believe my son is referring to — '

'A hound by the name of Boris?' asked Holmes.

The baron frowned. 'How did you know that?'

'The animal in question has been barking continuously ever since we arrived: indeed, when we first climbed down from our carriage, I distinctly heard someone admonish the creature, referring to it as Boris.' Looking back at Clemens, he said, 'I can imagine such a cacophony would be distracting indeed for a violinist.'

Clemens stared at him with new interest. 'It seems you are full of surprises, Herr Holmes. How did you know that I play the violin? May I ask who's been talking about me?'

'When one studies the violin as assiduously as you most assuredly do,' returned Holmes, 'the repeated pressure and friction upon one's fingertips eventually produces calluses. While they are not usually visible to the naked eye, they are most certainly unique to the task, and can be felt. I felt yours when we shook hands, and as an admittedly amateur violinist myself, recognized them immediately for what they were. I note also that your head tilts very slightly to the left, indicating neck pain, or certainly some degree of spinal discomfort — another unfortunate consequence of playing our chosen instrument for any length of time. However, I should think a properly adjusted shoulder rest would provide some relief.'

Clemens relaxed a little. 'Thank you. But this isn't just about concentration, sir. Look what the beast has done to my hand!'

Instinctively Watson stepped forward. 'Here — let me have a look.'

Clemens quickly drew it back. 'There's no need for that. I don't need a doctor to tell me that I won't be able to practise for at least two weeks.' He glared at his father. 'You'll have to have the thing put down.'

'I could never do that,' the baron replied. 'Boris is the only reminder Caroline has of her family. I won't take him away from her.'

Holmes arched one eyebrow. 'Caroline? That would be Fräulein Hertz, the daughter of the late doctor?'

The baron's response was a withering glance. 'I see you have been quite thoroughly briefed by the burgomaster.'

'He answered my questions,' replied Holmes. 'Nothing more.'

'Well, to answer the question you just asked me — yes, that is correct. I knew Caroline's father for many years. We took her in after he died, and have treated her as one of our own ever since.'

'Very commendable,' Holmes remarked. Then, turning back to Clemens: 'What happened, exactly? With the dog, I mean?'

'I spent the whole night studying,' replied the young man, 'without even taking time to sleep. When I came out of my room this morning, that horrible beast wound itself round my legs, and I tried to shoo it away. It bit me right down to the bone! I thought I would never be able to get my hand out of its mouth.'

'Maybe you scared him,' suggested the baron. 'You must have, because I've never known him to do such a thing before.'

'Why does everyone worship that beast?' demanded Clemens. Into the silence, the dog started barking again; deep, throaty barks that hinted at a dog of no small size. 'And there, do you hear?' he said. 'It never stops barking! Georg pretends he likes the thing because he takes an interest in its mistress.'

'Clemens,' snapped his father, 'you're being ridiculous. Caroline is like a sister to the pair of you.'

'Oh, don't be so naïve, Father. Georg is twenty years old, and I should be very surprised if eight months in Vienna haven't taught him the difference between an adopted sister and a potential conquest.'

For a heartbeat it appeared that the baron would reprimand him for making such a suggestion. Then he seemed to change his mind, and deflating, said instead, 'I'm sure our guests aren't interested in your ridiculous gossip.'

During the exchange, Holmes had wandered across to the window, ostensibly to give the two a modicum of privacy in which to discuss their differences. Now he found his attention taken by a young man and a girl out on the grounds, playing with a dog he took to be the troublesome Boris.

'On the contrary,' Holmes said, turning again and fixing Clemens with a gimlet eye. 'Tell me, would you say that your brother is . . . progressing in his amorous endeavours with Fräulein Hertz?'

'Good grief!' snapped the baron, stepping forward with his hands clenched angrily at his sides. 'What the devil kind of question is that? You are a guest here, sir. Please don't forget that!'

Clemens, however, saw no harm in Holmes's enquiry. 'I should say she treats him like the child he is.'

'Not especially well, then,' Holmes responded. 'Very well. Thank you for seeing us, Baron. We will trouble you no more.'

Frankenstein went to the door and tugged once on the tapestry bell pull hanging there. 'I hope you mean that, Herr Holmes,' he replied. 'Now, I'll have Bohmer show you out.'

* * *

As soon as the door closed behind them, Holmes descended the steps and set off for the landscaped gardens that he had seen from the day room window. Taken by surprise, Watson stopped partway toward the waiting barouche, then hurried along to the corner of the house in his wake.

'Holmes! What do you — ?'

The sight of the gardens silenced him. By any stretch, here was the single most appealing part of the castle. A manicured field rolled off toward a distant line of spruce trees, through which a series of gravel paths wound in long, lazy bends. Flowerbeds glowed with the colours of winter-flowering plants. Elsewhere stood rows of neatly clipped hedges and impressive examples of the topiarist's art: green-leafed elephants and tigers, butterflies and life-size men, pyramids and steeples.

In the centre of the lawn, a young couple were playing with a dog. It was the dog who first became aware of them. Immediately the creature started barking even more excitedly than it had before.

Wary of it, Watson felt in his pocket for the Webley. 'I say,' he said a trifle nervously, 'what do you suppose that brute is? I don't believe I've ever seen its like before.'

'I should say it is a cross between an Irish Wolfhound and a bloodhound,' Holmes replied. 'Why — does it remind you of anything?'

'You know perfectly well,' said Watson. 'And I thought never to encounter something as hideous as the Hound of the Baskervilles ever again.'

At just that moment Boris lunged forward and came bounding toward them, still barking at the top of his lungs. Watson froze, then made as if to draw his revolver, only to stop when Holmes snapped his name.

The dog rapidly hurtled closer. The sound of its paws drumming against the damp grass sounded more like an approaching army.

'Holmes . . . '

'Have a little faith, old friend.'

But faced with such a monster, slobber hanging from its gaping mouth in long, glutinous strings, Watson found faith in short supply.

At last the dog was finally close enough to leap — and leap it did. It threw itself at Watson, who tried manfully to fend it off by grabbing its forelegs. But the hound would not be denied — for whatever obscure motive, it intended to greet Watson as if he were a long-lost friend.

Almost before he realized it, Watson found himself wrestling good-naturedly with Boris, whose tail wagged ten to the dozen while the dog himself struggled desperately to lick Watson's face.

'There . . . there's a . . . a good . . . boy . . .'

'He seems to like you,' Holmes noted dryly.

'His . . . bark is certainly worse than his — yes, good boy, you're a very good boy — his bite. But how did you know he wouldn't tear me apart?'

'Though once employed as a hunting dog,' Holmes responded, 'the Irish wolfhound is not noted for its aggression. And while the bloodhound *can* have an aggressive streak, it is generally directed toward other animals.'

By this time the young couple had joined them. Beneath blond hair that was darkened and slicked flat to his head by macassar oil, the boy — he was about twenty — would have been handsome were it not for his features, which were rather too sharp, and his eyes, which were a frankly hostile dark blue. As he studied Holmes and Watson, he made no effort to disguise his obvious curiosity.

Older than him by perhaps a decade, his companion was slim and graceful; her triangular face, cheeks pink from the cold of the day, framed by gently waved black hair that was brushed back from her forehead and caught up in a heavy plait worn at the back of her head. In her elegant emerald-green kersey cape, she was as tall as her companion and regal in her bearing. But there was nothing of his arrogance about her; rather, she was simply confident and assured. Her eyes, a lighter shade of green than her cape, were large and good-humoured; her nose small, with flared nostrils; her mouth wide; her lips full; her jaw strong.

'How odd!' she noted when they were close enough. 'Boris normally shies away from strangers.'

'Does he . . . really?' Watson managed, still trying unsuccessfully to curb the dog's exuberance.

'Allow me to introduce us,' said Holmes, doffing his deerstalker. 'I am Sherlock Holmes, and this is Dr John Watson.'

'I assume you are guests of my father?' the boy asked coldly, making no effort to shake hands.

'We have just come from visiting him,' said Holmes. 'And as we were about to leave, we saw you both — and, of course, Boris here.'

'Then you know that I am Georg von Frankenstein, and this is Caroline Hertz.'

Watson bowed politely to Caroline. 'It is a pleasure to meet you, Fräulein.' Pointedly, he made no such claim to Georg.

Caroline, in turn, seemed impressed by Watson's good looks and manners — something that only made Georg's glare sharpen still more.

'Clemens told us that he was bitten this morning by your dog, Fräulein Hertz,' Watson continued. 'Though I must say,

Boris seems far from dangerous to me.'

'He isn't dangerous in the least,' she replied. 'He can be wary, certainly, and quite wonderfully obedient — usually, but he is never violent.'

'I can see he is obviously devoted to — '

'What brings you to our castle, anyway, Herr Holmes?' interrupted Georg.

'The murder of the unfortunate gravedigger,' said Holmes.

'Oh, that. What possible business could that be of ours?'

'In all probability, no business at all,' Holmes replied dismissively. 'But we have to explore all leads.'

'Are you seriously telling me you have come all the way from England just to investigate the death of a gravedigger?' asked the youngest Frankenstein, with something akin to disbelief.

Watson bristled at the tone and implication of his statement. 'Life is life, Herr Frankenstein, whether it belongs to a rich man or a pauper.'

'Well said,' commended Caroline before turning her attention to Holmes. 'Tell me,

Herr Holmes, how do you like Darmstadt so far?'

'Since we only arrived late last evening, it is still too early to tell,' Holmes replied. 'Now, if you will excuse us . . . '

'Oh, don't let us detain you,' Georg replied scathingly. 'And please pay our respects to Helder when next you see him — especially those of Caroline here.'

Caroline stiffened. 'Georg!'

'You know him well?' Holmes asked casually.

'He and my father were at university together, and have been friends ever since. But given half the chance, I'm sure he would prefer to think of himself as one of the family.'

Holmes pursed his lips. 'Would he, indeed?'

Bidding them farewell, he briskly retraced his steps toward the courtyard, with Watson in tow, but he hadn't gone more than a few yards when he had the feeling that they were being watched. Halting, he turned and looked up.

At one of the upper floor windows, the manservant, Bohmer, was staring down at them with an expression in his dark, slow-to-blink eyes that was impossible to read. For a moment longer they stared at each other. Then, unhurriedly, Bohmer let a curtain drop back across the window and vanished from sight.

★　★　★

As the castle fell behind them, Watson said, 'In the name of heaven, Holmes, why did we have to leave so abruptly?'

'No reason,' Holmes replied. 'I was merely reluctant to lose time in idle chatter that we might otherwise use for our inquiry.'

'What is that supposed to mean, 'idle chatter'?'

'Nothing.'

'It was not idle chatter I was exchanging with <u>Fräulein</u> Hertz, you know.'

'Watson, I never said it was.'

'No, but you certainly implied it.'

'Then for that I apologize. But you have already adopted one damsel in distress, remember.'

'My interest in Christina Klein is

purely professional.'

'Of course it is.'

'There you go again, saying one thing but implying another!'

'Watson . . . '

'All right, all right, I apologize, too. But it has been a long day, and my nerves are still frayed from being shot at.' After a slight pause he said, 'In any case, who says Caroline Hertz is in any distress?'

'She certainly seemed to find the attentions of young Georg rather less than gratifying.'

Watson felt in his pocket, checking that his service revolver was handy should they run into any trouble on the journey back. 'Changing the subject,' he said, 'when you interrogated the baron, it seemed to me that you had already established the link between Victor and his family.'

'I had.'

'How so?'

'A simple case of observation. When we first entered the castle, there were a series of portraits of all the previous barons hanging from the staircase wall. But the wall around two of them was a distinctly lighter shade than the rest, implying that the originals had been replaced by the portraits of two other persons, in slightly smaller frames. By noting the dates, I was able to compute that the missing portraits were most likely those of Victor and his father, Alphonse.'

'Well, one thing is certain,' said Watson. 'Our would-be assassin seems to have given up on us, at least for the moment. There's the town ahead.'

'Yes,' Holmes remarked, his tone curiously grim. 'Liebl, take us directly to the Rathaus, if you please! I think we should have a few more words with the burgomaster before we take this investigation any further.'

7

Gesundheit

Having finished organizing his desk for the next day's work — straightening his blotter, making sure his official stationery was set exactly parallel to the right edge of his desk and that his pens were standing to attention beside his bottle of Huber Company chromatic ink — Helder finally turned his attention to his beloved collection of automatons. He had just set one in motion — a seated, finely dressed woman with quill in hand, whose actions imitated the act of writing a letter — when the office door opened and Holmes strode inside with Watson close behind him.

Without preamble, Holmes said, 'Burgomaster, you have not been entirely truthful with us, have you?'

Helder frowned and hurriedly switched off the toy. Behind his thin wire-framed spectacles, his brown eyes looked thoroughly bewildered. 'I'm s-sorry . . . ?'

'Why didn't you tell us that the protagonists of Mrs Shelley's novel were based on real people? And before you deny it, I would hardly believe that a man in your position — and such a close and long-standing friend of the present baron — could be ignorant of such a fact.'

Helder was about to deny the accusation, then saw the futility in such a course. Hesitantly he said, 'Please understand, Herr Holmes — no one in Darmstadt talks of Victor Frankenstein or his branch of the family. We don't even acknowledge him, if we can help it.'

'So I believe. But if we are to continue with this investigation, I need your full cooperation. Should I find that factual information is being deliberately withheld from us, then Dr Watson and I will return to London without hesitation.'

'But you don't understand!' Helder said miserably. 'Our silence is intended to keep away the curse.'

'Curse?' echoed Watson.

The burgomaster stood up and paced

the room restlessly. 'That there was no creature or monster or whatever you want to call it hardly needs saying. But there *was* horror, of a sort, inasmuch as the family suffered a long series of tragedies that started two centuries ago. They began with the birth of Victor's father, Alphonse. Rumour had it that his birth was cursed because of . . . ' He drew a breath, then said quickly, ' . . . Dippel.'

'Who is Dippel?' demanded Watson.

Helder's expression sagged. 'You mean the baron didn't mention . . . ? Then it's not my place to — '

Turning away from him, Holmes asked, 'How much time do we need to pack our things, Watson?'

Playing along without having to be told, Watson pulled his watch from its fob pocket and checked the time in theatrical fashion. 'I should think — '

'All right, all right!' said Helder. 'But you must understand — I have the greatest respect for the Frankensteins, and it is difficult for me to discuss their secrets.'

'Quite,' said Holmes, adding casually,

'Oh, that reminds me — Fräulein Hertz sends her regards.'

Helder started. 'I . . . I beg your pardon?'

'Never mind,' said Holmes, taking a seat and watching the burgomaster as he stood with his back to the window. 'Now — to Dippel, if you please.'

Clearly unhappy about it, Helder said, 'Dippel — that is, Johann Conrad Dippel — was an alchemist and anatomist who was born in the late 1600s and lived at the castle, under the patronage and protection of the Frankenstein family. He was a somewhat . . . let us say controversial character who carried out many questionable experiments. Among these was thought transference, the attempted transference of souls from one body to another . . . He created an elixir of life with which he attempted — unsuccessfully — to buy the castle . . . And is known to have been an avid dissector of animals and humans. Boiling flesh and bones, he believed he had created a potion to exorcize demons, and on at least one occasion he was accused of consorting with demons himself.

'As you can imagine, he made many bitter enemies along the way. They condemned him as 'a vile devil who attempted wicked things'. And wicked they were. Paramount among them was his dream of creating man in his own image.'

'Blasphemy, in other words,' muttered Watson.

'Indeed,' agreed Helder, suddenly lowering his voice. 'And though it was never proved, the likelihood is that Alphonse Frankenstein was Dippel's illegitimate son.'

'Which would make Dippel Victor's grandfather,' muttered Watson.

'Yes. That, added to the rumour that he made a pact with the Devil in exchange for secret knowledge, is what probably inspired Mary Shelley's book.'

'But I thought it was her father's book — '

Holmes stood up suddenly. 'That last piece of information may prove to be much more important than we think,' he interrupted. 'Thank you, Burgomaster

— you have finally been helpful in the process of solving your case, though I suspect you will yet be of even greater assistance.'

'How so, Herr Holmes?'

'By accompanying us to the Freihof Brauberg.'

'The cemetery? What on earth do you want at the cemetery?'

'Under any other circumstances,' said Holmes, 'I would request that you provide us with an unrestricted exhumation permit. In this instance, however, I believe we would be wiser to dispense with legalities. After all, the fewer people who know about this business, the better.'

Helder's surprise registered in the raising of his grey-blond eyebrows. 'Exhumation — ? Who do you propose to exhume?'

'Any male who has died within the past . . . let us say, three months.'

'Is that really necessary? The townsfolk are superstitious enough as it is. You can hardly put the recently bereaved through this further horror.'

'Nevertheless, if we are to get to the bottom of this business, we must do so.'

'The next of kin might not give their permission,' Helder reminded him. 'It is perfectly within their right.'

'That is why I suggest we proceed in secret and not tell them.'

'Holmes!' breathed Watson, looking shocked to the core. 'As a doctor I cannot condone such a monstrously unethical suggestion!'

'Then permit me to explain my reasoning,' Holmes said coolly. 'Gentlemen, we are assuming — always a dangerous exercise in itself — that the murder and mutilation of the gravedigger was the first and only such crime here.'

'Are you saying it's not?'

'I am saying nothing of the sort, until the facts speak for themselves. But I *am* suggesting that the gravedigger may only have been the first *living* donor of limbs.'

'My God!' whispered Helder as he finally realized just what Holmes was saying. 'I . . . must consider this, Herr Holmes.'

'By all means,' replied Holmes. 'But do not tarry, Burgomaster. The trail is cold enough as it is. And if, as I suspect, your killer will strike again — and soon — then we had best act with all dispatch.'

'Yes . . . ' Helder murmured distract-edly. 'Yes . . . '

'Well, Burgomaster? Are you with us?'

'Is there no other way to test your theory?'

'I am afraid not.'

'Then . . . yes, sir, I am with you. God help me.' He took off his spectacles and polished them nervously. 'But we cannot undertake this deed in broad daylight.'

'Of course not. That is why we shall exhume the bodies under cover of dark-ness, tonight.'

Helder offered his hand, still clearly shaken by the prospect of what he had agreed to do. 'What, uh . . . what will you do in the meantime, gentlemen?'

'Do?' asked Holmes, as if the answer should be obvious. 'It has been a long and tiring day, Burgomaster. We shall return to the inn and have our supper.'

★　★　★

Holmes and Watson retired to their rooms to rest ahead of the coming night's work.

By mutual consent, they met again an hour later for supper, though the prospect of grave robbing had soured Watson's appetite. Klein fetched their meal in his usual brusque manner, almost throwing bowls of potato and beer soup down before them.

'So,' Holmes said in an undertone after the innkeeper had returned to the bar, 'did you have words with our rather less-than-genial host?'

'I did indeed,' Watson replied.

'And . . . ?'

'He wasn't even the slightest bit interested in the idea.'

'He doesn't believe you can help Christina to speak?'

Watson considered the question. As he did so, a tall, broad-shouldered man in his fifties came downstairs and went across to the bar. He handed a small stack of coins to Klein, then turned and left with his long black topcoat flowing around him.

'Well, it's not so much that,' he said at last. 'It's more as Helder said — he's not even willing to let me try!' He sipped his ale, which was far stronger than the beers back in England. 'That poor woman. She is absolutely broken, Holmes. If I could help her to speak again, allow her to really articulate her problems — '

'Hmmm,' Holmes replied, studying the door distractedly. 'By the way, what did you make of Castle Frankenstein?'

'It's a strange and poisonous place,' Watson said. 'If we are still here by the time of the next full moon, I wouldn't be at all surprised to see young Clemens turn into a werehound!'

'Or worse,' Holmes replied. 'Perhaps we should check to make sure he has a reflection. In any case, he did lie to us quite shamelessly today.'

'Clemens? What about?'

'You noticed, of course, the mud stains which were quite visible at the bottom of his trousers.'

'Oh, of course,' Watson replied sarcastically.

'They tell us that he did not spend the entire night in his room, as he told us.'

'Perhaps he went out to shut the dog up.'

'No, Watson. There was no need to go

outdoors. If you recall, his exact words were, 'I spent the whole night studying, without even taking time to sleep. When I came out of my room this morning, that horrible beast wound itself round my legs.''

'So what was Clemens up to, skulking around in the darkness?'

Before Holmes could reply, the door opened and Trautmann, the drunk with whom Holmes had fought the previous night, stamped inside, followed by two companions. The man broke stride when he saw Holmes and Watson eating supper, and the others almost walked into him. One was a short, portly man of about forty; the other taller, thinner and possibly a decade younger, with a shaggy blond moustache.

Watson stiffened, for he saw that Trautmann was carrying a rifle loosely in his left hand — an ill-used but nonetheless still-serviceable Mannlicher-Carcano carbine. All at once he realized who this morning's hidden marksman had been; and Trautmann's parting words — *Bloody foreigners! You haven't heard the last of me!* — took on a new and ominous significance to him.

He started to rise, intending to challenge the man, who was now leading his cronies to the bar, when Holmes said softly, 'Pass me the salt, will you, Watson?'

Sidetracked by the request, Watson said, 'What? Oh — here.' Again he started to rise.

'And the pepper, if you would be so kind.'

Glaring at him, Watson finally understood that he was being told in so many words to stay exactly where he was. 'Here,' he said unhappily, and set the pepper pot down harder than necessary.

Trautmann, meanwhile, put his rifle on the bar and ordered three tankards of ale. One of his companions — the short, portly one — muttered something and all three laughed harshly.

Holmes, touching his napkin to his mouth, asked loudly, 'Did you catch anything today, Herr Trautmann?'

The laughter died, and Trautmann turned to glower at him. 'What did you say?'

'I asked if you had caught anything today.'

'And what business is that of yours?'

Holmes rose and walked slowly toward him. 'Were I not the target of this morning's attempted murder, it would be no business of mine at all.'

It went very quiet in the inn. Then Trautmann said, 'That's a serious charge.'

'Attempted murder is a serious business,' replied Holmes. 'Or perhaps you only meant to scare us into leaving Darmstadt. Either way, you failed — quite miserably.'

Trautmann glanced from one of his friends to the other, then swaggered closer. His friends, flanking him on either side, came along with him, as if all three were joined by an invisible cord.

'Well,' said Trautmann, seemingly happy to play up to the inn's small audience, 'I claim no responsibility for whatever it is you're talking about. But there's no doubting that I owe you, *Inselaffe*.'

Trautmann's friends laughed at the derogatory term, which translated as 'island monkey'. Klein's few other customers exchanged nervous glances, shocked by the use of such an insult.

'Last night,' Trautmann went on, 'I was drunk out of my mind, and on my own.

Tonight I'm stone-cold sober, and I have Nagel and Zeigler here with me.'

Holmes smiled disarmingly. 'May I assume, then, that you are not going to turn yourselves over to the local authorities willingly? There are charges to answer, you know. You're lucky indeed that Liebl wasn't injured worse than he actually was.'

Trautmann and company looked at each other and smirked. Watson, jaw tightening, put his own napkin on the table and stood up.

'Fancy your chances, do you?' asked Trautmann.

'*Gesundheit*,' said Holmes by way of reply.

Trautmann's expression relaxed. 'What was that?'

Even as he asked the question, Holmes flung the contents of the pepper pot into the faces of the three Germans. As they reared back, coughing and clutching at their burning eyes, Holmes immediately stepped forward, wrapped his right arm around Trautmann's throat, tucked his right leg behind both of Trautmann's, and with the minimum of leverage threw the man hard to the floor.

Watson, meanwhile, had planted himself before the lanky man — Trautmann's earlier flick of the eyes had identified him as Nagel — and easily blocked the unimaginative jab the fellow threw in his direction. He responded with a punch of his own, which clipped Nagel's jaw and sent him staggering backwards. He followed his opponent across the room, intending to finish him quickly, but ran straight into a return blow instead. For a moment he ears rang; then as his vision cleared, he saw Nagel trying to crowd him, and launched a second punch that dropped his opponent on the spot.

That just left Zeigler. The portly man had come up hard against the bar, where he quickly made a grab for the rifle. Klein was faster, and deftly tore the weapon out of his reach. Thinking fast, Zeigler swept up an empty bottle instead, intending to use it as a weapon. As he came at Holmes with the bottle held high for a clubbing blow, Holmes dropped to a crouch and, using both fists, planted a withering double punch to his opponent's sternum. Zeigler made an awful wheezing sound and then stumbled away again, bending double and choking for air, the bottle dropping from his fingers to shatter on the floor. Amazingly, the entire altercation had taken no more than five seconds.

Klein bellowed, 'Enough!' And to underline the word, he worked the bolt on the rifle and covered the combatants. 'You,' he said, addressing Holmes. 'You have a grievance with these men?'

'They tried to shoot us!' breathed Watson.

'All right. You there — Bachmeier!' snapped Klein, jabbing the rifle at a nearby customer. 'Go and fetch Oberwachtmeister Reiniger. He can charge them and lock them away until they can stand trial. As for this rifle . . . I suppose this is what they call evidence.'

Stumbling back to his feet, Trautmann swore. 'You can't do this!'

'I think you'll find that I can do anything I please,' Klein replied. 'And if you don't like it, you can take it up with the burgomaster.'

8

The Body Snatcher

Muffled against the damp midnight night air, Holmes and Watson arrived at the moon-silvered cemetery gates to discover the burgomaster and a very nervous-looking Liebl already waiting for them. Helder was carrying a closed lantern, Liebl a shovel and a crowbar. Neither man looked especially pleased to be there. Fortunately, the cemetery lay on the outskirts of the town, so there was little chance that they would be observed at such an hour.

'Herr Holmes,' Helder greeted in a harsh whisper. 'Are you absolutely sure we need to go through with this?'

Holmes nodded. 'Were it not crucial to my investigation, I would be more than happy to call it off,' he replied, speaking softly himself. 'Unfortunately, it is essential.'

With one final guilty glance around,

Helder unlocked the gates and pushed them open. They swung inward with a low grinding sound that seemed much louder than it really was. With footsteps crunching on the gravel path, they entered the cemetery, Liebl closing the gates behind them.

'Where do we begin?' whispered the burgomaster.

'You have the records I requested?' Holmes said.

'The names of all the men who have died and been interred here over the last three months, between the ages of twenty and forty. There were just three.'

'Then our work should soon be done. Please, Burgomaster, lead us to the first name on your list.'

As they made their way deeper into the cemetery, Watson thought back to their earlier fight. While waiting for the local man, Bachmeier, to fetch the constable, he had felt eyes on him; and when he'd turned, it was to see Christina Klein standing on the open staircase, looking down at him. Foolishly, he had immediately finger-brushed his hair back into place and straightened his crooked tie.

By then she had reached the foot of the stairs and come towards him, her face a picture of concern. It was only when she took out a tiny creased handkerchief and reached up to blot his mouth that he realized his lip had split, and that there was blood on his chin.

As Christina tended to him, he looked down into her eyes. This time she didn't look away, and he saw that she had been crying. He opened his mouth to ask her what was wrong, when Klein barked, 'Christina! What do you think you're playing at? Tidy up this mess!'

The sound of his voice made her flinch, and she turned away at once and set to work, cleaning up.

Now, the cemetery closed in around them. Most of it was overgrown, and the air carried with it a sweet smell, as of honeysuckle. That, Watson thought, would doubtless be the rhododendrons young Maria Richter had been picking the day she witnessed the murder of Mauritz Färber.

Then Helder halted at a cold-looking stone mausoleum covered with moss and ivy. The arched entrance was enclosed by two narrow iron gates, held shut by a heavy padlock. Above the gates, engraved in the weatherworn stone, read the legend:

Frankenstein

'The Frankenstein vault!' hissed Watson.

'Yes,' said Helder. 'For more than a century, the Frankensteins have been laid to rest here.'

They pushed on, until at last the burgomaster came to a halt in what appeared to be a more modern, and tidier, section of the burial ground. 'Here is the first of them,' he said, indicating a relatively new headstone.

The deceased's name was Abelard Kappel, and he had died a month earlier at the age of thirty-four, cause of death chronic nephritis. Liebl looked up at Holmes, who gave one brusque nod. With another glance at the burgomaster, Liebl licked his lips and began to dig.

It seemed to take forever. After a while Liebl stood back and ran a sleeve across his forehead. 'I think Herr Färber earned every pfennig of his pay, digging earth as hard as this,' he muttered.

'Here,' said Watson, anxious both to occupy himself and get this wretched business over with as soon as possible. 'Let me have a go.'

As he continued digging, Holmes looked at Helder and asked, 'How much *did* you pay Färber, anyway?'

'Does it matter?'

'I would not have asked, otherwise.'

Helder stamped his feet against the seeping chill. 'It is a lowly position. His salary reflected that.'

'Did he work any additional jobs?'

'No. The man was largely illiterate, and as I told you before, most people gave him a wide berth, believing it to be bad luck to have anything to do with him. Indeed, I sometimes felt he was not even qualified to dig graves.'

'But he gave you no cause for complaint?'

'No. He took his duties seriously enough.'

The work continued, and slowly but surely the pile of dirt beside the grave grew to a low mound. When Watson finally stepped back to regain his breath, Holmes took his turn. Shortly thereafter he was rewarded by a solid, hollow thump, as the shovel hit the lid of the coffin beneath it.

Silence settled over the graveyard, broken only by the scurrying of nocturnal animals through the undergrowth and the sudden startled cry of a rabbit snared by a wolf. Then Liebl eased himself down into the hole and began to prise at the coffin lid with the crowbar.

'Careful, now,' muttered Watson, throwing a meaningful glance at Holmes. 'Let us at least try to treat the dead with some respect.'

At last there was a screech of wood, and Liebl pulled back the lid. Holmes took the lantern from Helder and raised it high. Shadows yawed sideways, as if chased away by the light. Then —

Helder reared back from the sight and hurriedly crossed himself.

'Good God!' said Watson.

'What devilry is this?' breathed the burgomaster. 'The coffin . . . it . . . it's *empty*.'

'As I suspected,' Holmes said softly.

'B-but the body — ' began Helder.

Paying him no mind, Holmes said briskly, 'What is the next name on your list?'

'Not so fast, Holmes,' said Watson. 'We should rebury Herr Kappel's coffin before we move on to the next.'

'Yes, yes, but we still have much to do, and relatively little time in which to do it.'

'Nevertheless,' Watson said firmly, 'we will reinter this grave first.'

Fortunately for Holmes, whose only interest was to confirm his suspicions, it was easier to fill the grave than it had been to excavate it. They shared the work in silence, and then Helder led them to the second grave on his list. This one belonged to Walther Sandt, who had died at the age of forty from a blood clot on the brain. This grave, too, was empty.

There was almost no need to exhume the third coffin, but they did it anyway, and this one was also unoccupied.

'I begin to make sense of this business,' Holmes mused as they retraced their steps to the cemetery gates. 'I suspect that Herr Färber was involved in body-snatching.'

'What?' gasped Helder.

'By your own admission, Burgomaster, you paid him a lowly salary. He had no other form of employment, and was largely shunned by those around him. And yet he could often be found buying drinks for his fair-weather friends. Clearly he had an additional source of income.'

'From grave-robbing?' asked Helder.

'That I cannot say,' replied Holmes, 'since grave-robbing is a very different proposition to body-snatching. That the bodies were taken, there is no doubt. As to whether or not they were robbed after they were disinterred, we do not know. It is, of course, too late to interrogate Färber himself, but I would strongly advise that you pay whoever replaces him more generously.'

Ignoring this, Helder said, 'But . . . who would buy the bodies?'

'The snatching of bodies is nothing new,' Holmes replied. 'Ever since man has tried to learn the workings of the human body in order to cure its many ailments, there has been a buoyant market for the so-called 'resurrection men'. Do you have any medical schools in the vicinity?'

'N-no.'

'And anatomy is beyond the remit of the Technical University?'

'Of course.'

'Then we must look elsewhere. Färber was illiterate, so it is unlikely he would have kept records of his enterprise. And if he stole any items of value with which the bodies were buried, we can safely say that he disposed of them very shortly thereafter. But the fact remains that someone had need of these cadavers. But for what purpose, other than dissection?'

Watson grimaced. 'Cannibalism?'

Liebl made a sick, choking sound.

'Clay,' said Holmes.

Watson shook his head. 'This is no time to speak in riddles,' he said irritably.

'Then I draw your attention to the legend of Prometheus,' Holmes replied. 'According to the likes of Sappho and Aesop, Prometheus played a significant part in the creation of humanity, fashioning humans out of — '

' — clay,' finished Watson. 'You're suggesting that these poor missing unfortunates

. . . they provided the 'clay' that Färber's customer needed to create new life? The spare parts? Holmes, that is ridiculous.'

'Nevertheless,' said Holmes, 'you know my tenet; when you have eliminated the impossible, whatever remains, however improbable, must be the truth. It certainly explains why Färber's leg was removed, and suggests a purpose for the items that were stolen from Saint Corbinian's. Unfortunately, the very fact that three of the most recent cadavers to be interred here are missing implies that someone has been . . . harvesting them. After all, a single corpse would not be sufficient for a major surgical experiment, which would require ongoing replacement parts.'

'You're not suggesting — ' Watson began

'The kind of experiment that Mary Shelley describes in her book?' Holmes finished. 'Why not?'

'So this giant who killed Färber — was he the man who was buying the bodies, do you think? Or perhaps a relative of one of the unfortunates, who discovered what was going on and decided to confront him about it? The girl, Maria Richter, said they appeared to be arguing, remember — and the burgomaster suggested in his letter that Färber had been strangled by someone in a fury.'

'True — but it could just as easily have been a falling-out among thieves, perhaps over shares of the money. In any case, I rather fancy that Färber's killer, and the customer who bought the bodies from him, are two different people. And as dangerous as the killer undoubtedly is, I believe Färber's customer is the more dangerous of the two. Who knows what he's up to?'

'Who, indeed?'

'That is what we need to find out,' Holmes said briskly. He checked the time. 'First thing tomorrow, I believe we shall pay Dr Richter another visit.'

9

A Dead Man Walking

In the lobby of Saint Corbinian's the following morning, Holmes and Watson were fortunate to encounter Frau Vogler again. The almoner was sorry to say that Dr Richter was still absent from work, but that she had made enquiries at the Technical University, and yes, they too had suffered one or two minor thefts over the past few months.

'Did they tell you what had been stolen?' asked Holmes.

'Equipment,' she replied, 'much of it too complicated to pronounce or remember. But I do recall one item — it was called an 'influence machine'. Does that mean anything to you, Herr Holmes?'

Holmes pondered it for a moment. 'I believe it does, yes,' he answered at length. 'Thank you, Frau Vogler. You have been of great help. I have one final question, and then we shall leave you to go about your work. Do you by any chance have Dr Richter's address?'

'You're already there.' She smiled. 'He lives here, on the hospital grounds. We have a garden of sorts at the rear of the hospital. Dr Richter and his family live in the cottage on the far side. You can't miss it.'

As they walked the length of the hospital, headed for a set of doors at the far end, Holmes said, 'You know, of course, Watson, what an influence machine is?'

'I can't say that I've ever heard the expression before.'

'It is another name for the more familiar Wimshurst machine.' Wimshurt machines were used to generate and build charges of static electricity by means of two parallel but counter-rotating discs.

'You are implying, of course, that the charge generated by such a machine could be sufficient to stimulate life in flesh that was once dead?' said Watson.

'I am indeed,' replied Holmes. 'After all, we have all seen experiments involving dead frogs that appear to come back to life when an electrical charge is passed through them. If the charge is of sufficient power, who is to say we cannot turn that temporary state of affairs into a permanent one?'

The doors at the far end of the corridor opened out onto a stone staircase, beyond which stood a large field set around a central, now somewhat overgrown, flowerbed. Sure enough, on the far side there stood a small whitewashed cottage with black-painted *fachwerk* beams and small casement windows.

Holmes and Watson followed a crooked path to the front door, where Holmes used the head of his cane to rap at one of the panels. A few seconds later the door opened, and they found themselves being scrutinized by a tall, broad-shouldered man in his fifties. Holmes recognized him at once. Heavily featured, with short blond hair that presently looked somewhat dishevelled, and a strong, square jaw, Lars Richter was the same man he had seen coming down from the upper floors of the inn the night before and giving money to Johann Klein before leaving.

'Dr Richter?' said Holmes, extending his hand.

After a moment's hesitation, Richter took it. His own was massive, and it was hard to believe that such a hand could possess the necessary lightness of touch so often required in surgery.

'I am Sherlock Holmes, and this is my companion, Dr Watson.'

Richter allowed himself a brief twitch of his thin, sour lips. 'I've been expecting you, gentlemen. They told me at the hospital that you had turned up yesterday, asking after me.'

'I wonder if we might ask you some questions?' said Holmes.

Richter studied them through hooded pale blue eyes, then said, 'If you must.' He stood aside and allowed them into a small untidy parlour with a low ceiling.

'I should also like to question your wife and daughter, if I may,' said Holmes, as he gave the room what appeared to be a cursory examination.

'I'm afraid that's impossible,' Richter

replied, moving to the centre of the heavily patterned carpet. 'My wife has taken Maria away to her parents in Malmö for a few days. With all the business at the cemetery she thought it best, and I agreed with her. However, I shall be happy to answer your questions.'

'You have been absent from work these past few days,' said Holmes.

'I've been . . . unwell.'

'May I ask how long you have lived here, at the hospital?'

'Close on five years, now. I took over following the death of Dr Hertz.'

'So your little Maria has lived for almost five years near the diseased, the dying and the demented,' Holmes mused. 'Does she ever have nightmares?'

'Occasionally. Every child does, you know. As do adults.'

'Does she have many friends?'

'She prefers her own company.'

'Being a solitary child, then, she must have developed some imagination.'

Richter's expression hardened. 'My daughter doesn't lie to me.'

'I have no doubt about that, Dr

Richter. But it could be that, in the horror of the moment, what she saw was somehow . . . embellished in the retelling. As you can imagine, even the smallest detail is important. We must cast the emotional response aside and focus solely upon the facts as they were, not as we remember them.'

Richter studied him thoughtfully. 'As a man of science, I understand your reasoning, Herr Holmes. But Maria is a level-headed girl. Imaginative, certainly — but not given to flights of fancy or 'embellishment', as you call it. The afternoon she saw the giant, it was overcast and the light was not good. Nevertheless, she said he was the ugliest thing she'd ever seen. He was exceptionally tall, as judged against the gravedigger, who himself was not short, and he walked with a very pronounced limp. In short, he had about him the appearance of a dead man walking.'

'But that, as we know, is impossible,' Holmes pointed out.

'And I only used it as a turn of phrase. As far as I am concerned, what she really saw was a drunken tramp with some kind of affliction.'

'Drunk, because he left behind him a smell as of aged whiskey,' said Holmes, quoting Helder's letter.

'Precisely. In any case, no one has seen him since. I imagine he is long gone by now. And frankly, sir, the apprehension of murderers is not my concern.'

'And yet your wife thought it safer to take Maria away from Darmstadt — to take her a quite considerable distance, all the way back to your native Sweden.'

'What are you trying to imply, Herr Holmes?'

'Nothing,' said Holmes innocently. 'And I fully understand your lack of interest in the identity of Färber's killer. At the moment you are, I believe, more concerned with thievery.'

Richter nodded. 'You are referring to the break-ins at our pharmacy,' he said. 'Most inconvenient. The burgomaster sets our budget, you see, and as a consequence we can hardly afford to run Saint Corbinian's as it is. We certainly can't afford to restock after every theft.'

'Do you suspect anyone in particular?'

Richter showed him a disparaging smile. 'An amateur chemist, perhaps?' he suggested mockingly. 'A practical joker with a very poor sense of humour? How should I know?'

'Of course,' said Holmes. 'I have just one final question, if I may.'

'Very well.'

'When do you expect your wife and daughter back?'

Richter stared at him for a moment, then made a meaningless gesture with one hand. 'Soon, I am sure.'

'Then good day to you, Herr Doctor. You have been most helpful.'

As they retraced their steps to the waiting barouche, Watson shook his head. 'I must confess,' he said, 'this business makes no sense at all, unless one is prepared to throw caution to the wind and believe in fairy stories.'

'And yet the evidence — '

'I know, I know. But Holmes, I ask you again . . . are you really convinced that someone has taken to stealing body parts in order to stitch them together like . . . like

Barnum's mermaid?'

'I thought the mermaid was real.'

'Hmmm! Then maybe I should examine your brain!'

'Not a proposition I can accept, my dear fellow. However, I believe I can offer you a distraction that may well prove even more illuminating.'

'Oh?'

'Yes,' said Holmes. 'We are going to take a closer look at the Frankenstein family vault.'

Watson broke stride and gaped at him. 'We are what? Whatever for? In any case, I doubt very much that the baron will allow that.'

'That is precisely why we are not going to ask him.'

'Holmes — !'

'Of course, if you prefer to miss out on what may well be a thrilling turning-point in our investigation . . . '

'You know I would never do that. But even so, Frankenstein will be furious if he finds out — and the burgomaster may well have a few choice words for you himself.' He sighed heavily. 'What is the point of breaking into the Frankenstein vault, anyway?'

'To verify another theory.'

'Which is?'

'Seventeen ninety-seven,' said Holmes.

Watson pondered for a moment. 'The last time Britain was invaded by the French,' he muttered at last. 'At Fishguard.'

'There is little I can teach you about history, I see,' Holmes returned. 'But it was also the year Alphonse Frankenstein died. The year Victor Frankenstein's wife Elizabeth died alongside her child. And the same year Mary Shelley was born.' He climbed into the barouche. 'The cemetery,' he instructed Liebl.

The little clerk sighed. 'Again?'

'I'm afraid so.'

As the barouche moved off, Watson said, 'Go on, Holmes.'

'The question we need to answer now is why Mary chose to tell Victor's story. According to the baron, his life was of no great significance. Why not tell Dippel's story instead?'

'I still don't see what you're getting at.'

'Put all the elements together, Watson. Mary wrote her book after visiting Castle Frankenstein. We know her story uses themes from a local legend, but it also closely resembles the book written by her father, William Godwin. And finally, Mary was born the exact same year as Elizabeth's stillborn child.'

Watson began to look uneasy. 'Don't tell me you are considering — '

'On the contrary, old friend, I am! Who is to say Godwin's child was not the stillborn one? He could have sought to relieve his grief by making the trip to Germany. He could have met the Frankenstein family, who could in turn have entrusted him with Elizabeth's child in return for the promise that he would raise her in England as his own. This would terminate Alphonse's line of descent, and effectively remove Victor's branch of the family for good and all. Godwin visiting Darmstadt would also explain why so much of *St. Leon* is based on the same local legend that his daughter used years later.'

'But Holmes, if you're right . . . that

would make Mary Shelley Victor's daughter!'

'We'll know that for certain if the coffin of Elizabeth and her child contains only one body.'

'Well, yes, but . . . Holmes, I have deep reservations about this.'

'Then stay here.'

But Watson could not leave Holmes to work alone. When the coach came to a halt before the cemetery gates, Holmes stepped down and spent a short time inspecting the place. It looked no less bleak in daylight than it had at midnight.

'We shan't be long,' Holmes told Liebl. Then he entered the cemetery with Watson at his side.

Cautiously they worked their way through the graveyard. Mist floated sluggishly around their shins, and a stray breeze sent brittle autumn-brown leaves scuttling from one side of the gravel path to the other.

At last they came to the Frankenstein family vault. Without needing to be told, Watson turned and kept a watch while Holmes, who never travelled without a small pick and tension wrench, bent and set to work picking the padlock that held the gates shut. A few seconds passed, and then the padlock yielded with a soft click. Holmes swung the gates open, then turned his attention to the heavy oak door that entombed the Frankenstein dead.

This time his efforts with the tension wrench and a small 'rake', which contained a number of distinct ridges, seemed to take forever. Watson's eyes were constantly on the move, but still everything appeared quiet.

'Look,' he hissed at length, 'perhaps this isn't such a good idea after — '

He was interrupted by a click, and then Holmes straightened back to his full height and, turning the apple-sized iron door handle, swung the door itself open.

A draught of stale, dusty air immediately assailed their nostrils. Clamping handkerchiefs over their mouths and noses, they went inside.

In the darkness directly before them, something small and hairy scuttled off with a startled squeak. Awkwardly, Watson lit a match and held it high.

Uncertain light filled a long, narrow mausoleum with a stone floor and shelves set in each wall that were wide enough to hold the coffins of the dead.

'Hold that flame steady,' muttered Holmes. 'These dust-covered nameplates are difficult enough to read as it is.'

Before the match could burn down to his fingertips, Watson extinguished it and lit a new one. Cupping the flame, he followed Holmes deeper into the vault, Holmes pausing at each coffin to read its inscription.

As they neared the far end, Holmes finally stopped at a dusty, timeworn coffin with a brass nameplate across which crouched an enormous black spider. With a grimace, Holmes brushed the spider away. It fell to the floor and scurried away on legs as thick as black as shoelaces.

Rubbing the dust from the nameplate, he read the inscription:

Elizabeth von Frankenstein
und
Unbenannte Kind

They exchanged a look.

Elizabeth von Frankenstein and Unnamed Child.

Watson licked his lips and was about to whisper something, when the second match burned down to his skin. Hastily he fished out and lit a third. Wavering light played across the coffin lid. Holmes reached over and grasped it by the edges, then gently loosened it and lifted it free. The wood made a hollow, scratchy sound that bounced off the dusty stone walls.

He tilted the lid away from them. A wave of stale air rose from the darkness beneath. Watson moved closer and held the match higher.

The skeletal remains of a single adult were its sole contents. Of the child there was not even the faintest trace.

Watson whispered, 'Do you . . . ' He had to clear his throat and start again. 'Do you think the baron knows about this?'

Thoughtfully, Holmes replaced the lid. 'I should be very surprised if he didn't. But it would be in his interests to say nothing about it. Such secrets are a perfect seed for intrigue, bitterness — and crime.'

They went back outside, where Watson turned his collar up against a chill that had little to do with the inclement weather. 'What are you planning to do now, Holmes?' he asked as Holmes relocked the door, then the gates. 'I have a suggestion.'

Holmes eyed him enquiringly. 'Please don't keep it to yourself.'

'I think we should go back to the castle on the pretext of checking on Clemens's hand. I must say it could stand to be examined, anyway. And perhaps while we're there, you could — '

'Perhaps while we're there,' Holmes cut in, 'you could renew your acquaintance with Fräulein Hertz, is that it?'

Watson stiffened. 'How — '

'Watson, I am well aware of your reputation with the fairer sex,' Holmes stated. 'That women on no less than five of the seven continents have succumbed to your charms. My goodness, you have mentioned it often enough! So we both know why you really want to go back to the castle.'

'Well . . . so what if I do happen to pay my respects to Fräulein Hertz while we're there?'

'You puzzle me, Watson. There is so much mystery at hand, so many stones still to turn, and yet you would ignore everything just to flirt with a woman half your age?'

Watson's mouth tightened. 'Holmes,' he grated, 'this conversation is over.'

'Why? Because the truth hurts?'

Watson wanted to tell him that what really hurt was to have loved and lost, not once but twice; that for some men — for most men — the company of a woman was a pleasant diversion, something to be enjoyed and even cherished. But of all the things he understood, Holmes would never understand that. In matters of the heart, and when it came to the social graces, he was as much an automaton as the burgomaster's clockwork toys. You wound him up and he detected . . . but he could feel nothing more than the thrill of the chase.

Watson wanted to tell this to Holmes, but in the end he said only, 'You go off to see what stones you can turn, and I will obey the dictates of my vocation and use the excuse of checking on Clemens's injury to see what else I can unearth about this business. We shall meet later at the inn.'

Holmes, realizing that he had spoken out of turn and in some way upset his companion, merely nodded. 'As you wish,' he said softly. 'And by all means take the carriage. It is but a short walk back into Darmstadt from here.'

10

Where is Boris?

'I've told you, Doctor, it is nothing,' Clemens said testily. He had agreed to see Watson in the day room, until he heard the supposed reason for the doctor's visit.

'Nevertheless,' Watson responded, 'you really should let me examine your hand, otherwise you face the risk of serious infection. Do you know the dog's history at all?'

'Maybe you should ask Caroline,' Clemens replied. 'You'll doubtless find her in the library.'

Watson felt his heart beat a little faster. 'Perhaps I — '

'Boris had no illnesses,' said Georg, entering unannounced.

Watson turned to face the arrogant young man. 'Had?' he repeated.

'He disappeared yesterday, shortly after

your visit,' Georg explained, coming further into the room. 'I spent most of the day and evening looking for him around the castle and the forest below. Caroline is very upset — and for that reason alone, I would suggest you reconsider your intention to question her.'

'Good riddance, I say!' Clemens said venomously. 'That animal was rabid.'

It was a possibility — albeit an unlikely one — that Watson was quick to exploit. 'Which is precisely why I should examine your — '

'You've no reason to blame Boris for your little scratch, Clemens,' Georg sneered. 'You deliberately provoked him.'

Clemens reacted as if struck. 'Are you saying I *wanted* him to bite me?'

For a moment they squared up to each other, and fearing that they might actually come to blows, Watson moved quickly to intercede. 'Was Boris in the habit of wandering away from the castle?' he asked, hoping to defuse the situation.

Clemens shrugged, and without taking his eyes off Georg said, 'He was tied to the whims of his mistress.'

Georg nodded, as if confirming something to himself. 'Well, you always did want to be rid of that creature,' he accused. 'Now you've got your wish. But you've no idea the grief his loss will cause.'

'I'm sure you'll get something out of it,' Clemens returned icily. 'Now you can comfort Caroline and finally be her knight in shining armour.'

'Don't take that tone with me!'

'Why shouldn't I? And who are you to lecture me, anyway? Attempting to court the woman we've always treated more like our sister! Really, what have you learned at university?'

'Gentlemen,' said Watson, 'I believe this is hardly the place for me just now. I'm sorry you would not allow me to examine your hand, Clemens, but should you change your mind, you will find me at — '

'Yes, yes,' Georg muttered dismissively, still glaring at his brother.

For Watson, that was the last straw. 'I'll see myself out.'

But he had no intention of leaving just yet. As soon as he closed the door behind him, he glanced around, then hurried across the vaulted lobby toward a door flanked by tarnished suits of armour. The door stood slightly ajar, and the moment he crossed the threshold he knew he had found the library to which Georg had referred. The room was stacked from floor to high panelled ceiling with book-stuffed shelves, and exuded an unmistakable smell of antiquity. A huge fireplace occupied the facing wall, around which had been set comfortable chairs and ornate hexagonal tables. Caroline was standing before the wall to his left, seemingly lost in her study of so many leather-bound spines.

Watson looked at her and was struck by just how completely opposite she was to poor Christina Klein. Where he felt only compassion toward Christina, there was something about Caroline that stirred his very soul.

Again he heard Holmes's accusation — *You would ignore everything just to flirt with a woman half your age?* — and felt a stab of guilt. Was that really what he had in mind — a flirtation? Had he really become so desperate for female companionship since the death of his second wife?

It occurred to him then that it might be best simply to turn around and leave before Caroline even knew he was there. But almost before he realized it, he cleared his throat and she turned quickly — and recognizing him, seemed flustered.

'Forgive me, Fräulein Hertz,' he said, closing the door softly behind him. 'I didn't mean to startle you.'

'Dr Watson,' she said, her tone difficult to decipher. Was she pleasantly surprised to see him, or irritated by his sudden interruption? 'I . . . you must forgive me. I'm so used to having this room to myself.'

'The library?' he asked. 'I should have thought this to be one of the most-used rooms in the castle.'

'Not this one. The Frankensteins never visit this room. It's usually locked.'

'But . . . a library such as this . . . '

'There are two in the castle,' she explained. 'But this one is special.' She stepped to one side and indicated that he should examine the contents of the shelf she had been inspecting. To his surprise he found himself looking at a bewildering array of different editions of Mary Shelley's *Frankenstein*, plus other works by her and her father, including *St. Leon*.

'I say,' he breathed appreciatively. Coming closer, he pulled one particular title from the shelf and turned its pages almost reverently.

'It's a first edition from 1818,' said Caroline. 'You can tell because Mary Shelley's name is missing, do you see? It didn't appear on the book until it was reprinted.'

'It must be close to priceless, I should imagine,' Watson replied, putting it back where he'd found it. 'But . . . why would anyone assemble such a collection? Especially in view of the damage it has caused the Frankensteins?'

'I've never dared ask the baron,' she replied. 'But it could be that the family tried to reduce the number of books in circulation by buying up as many copies as they could. They have always been especially keen to limit the book's readership, especially in this part of the world.'

'It certainly sounds like the best explanation.'

'I come here quite often,' she confided. 'This room has such a wonderful feeling of solitude.'

'Then I'm very sorry to have disturbed you. But . . . well, I heard that Boris has gone missing and . . . I hope nothing has happened to him and that he'll soon come bounding home again.'

'I certainly hope so, too. I like to think that I'll always have him near me.' As much as she didn't want to show it, her voice caught a little as she said it.

'Georg said he spent the night looking for him.'

'Yes. He came back very late and was so ashamed to have returned empty-handed.'

He frowned. 'Going into the forest at night might not be the best of ideas at the moment. There is a murderer loose out there, you know.'

Her green eyes widened. 'Do you

suppose he is still in the area? Everyone assures me that he has moved on by now, whoever he was.'

'Well, until we know for sure, caution is advisable.'

Caroline seemed to brighten suddenly. 'I was about to go for a walk in the garden. Would you . . . I mean, would you care to accompany me?'

'I would consider it a privilege,' said Watson, meaning it.

She was about to say more, but stopped as the sound of an approaching coach drifted to them from the courtyard. Crossing to the window, they were just in time to see a carriage pull up beside the barouche. When the coachman opened the door, the burgomaster climbed down. Nodding a perfunctory acknowledgement to Liebl, who was standing beside the barouche's team, he mounted the stone steps leading to the front door.

'Helder,' she said, stepping back from the window. 'He's the last person we want to see just now. We'll wait a few minutes until he's settled in the drawing room with the baron, then go out for that walk.'

★ ★ ★

In the drawing room, Baron Frankenstein said tiredly, 'Helder, I still can't believe you brought Sherlock Holmes here with a request to dig up a past that was better left buried!'

The burgomaster, standing before the fireplace like a schoolboy being reprimanded by his headmaster, looked thoroughly miserable. 'I thought it was in the best interests of the family,' he said, adding earnestly, 'I did it in the name of our friendship.'

'Did you, indeed?' demanded Frankenstein. But almost immediately he calmed down. 'Did you, Simon?' he asked in a softer tone. 'Even though I never wanted to hear the name of Victor Frankenstein ever again?'

Helder made a helpless gesture with his hands. 'Can't you see, Karl? That is precisely why I called Holmes in! If we had called in the federal authorities to investigate Färber's death, the name of Frankenstein would have been on the lips of every man, woman and child in the state — maybe the whole world! I was only trying to save the Frankenstein name from being besmirched yet again.'

Frankenstein continued to stare through the window. 'Someone put you up to this, didn't they, Simon?' he said after a while.

Helder took off his spectacles and gave them a quick polish. 'I'm sure I don't know what you mean.'

'And I am sure that you do. You would never have taken it upon yourself to seek the assistance of the great Sherlock Holmes without consulting me first. And yet that is precisely what you did. Unless,' he added, turning around at last, 'it was suggested to you by someone else.'

Helder blustered, 'Are you saying I cannot think for myself, Karl? If so, you do me a grave injustice.'

'I'm saying that you and I have known each other since university. We have never lied to each other, but something tells me you are lying to me now. So, tell me — was it really the best interests of my family name that prompted your action? Because if it was, then you may well have brought us more trouble than we had to begin with!'

★ ★ ★

With a coquettish smile, Caroline took Watson's arm, and together they strolled along the gravel paths that scored the castle's delightful garden. 'It's such a pleasure having someone to talk to,' she confessed. 'Especially someone from England. It can get lonely here.'

'Even with Georg constantly by your side?'

She shrugged. 'He's on the brink of manhood. That, I think, has filled his mind with romantic ideas. But to me he will always be my little brother.'

Watson was secretly glad to hear it. 'They're very different, Georg and Clemens,' he remarked.

'Clemens lives in a world of his own. He's sensitive, so I think he prefers it that way. In his own world he has at least some control over what happens. In the real world he has none.'

'And Georg?'

'Georg can be . . . mercurial. But he has charm, when he chooses to show it, and talent.'

'The burgomaster said your father and he were friends.'

'They were. We arrived in Darmstadt when I was rather young. Doctors were rare in this region back then, and vital to the community. The baron took us under his wing and looked after us.' She fell silent.

'And Boris?' Watson asked.

'Boris loved my father. They were inseparable. I suppose Boris helped me remember my father after he died. He never left my side — until now. In the words of your great poet, Shakespeare, I can only hope that like a broken limb united, I'll grow stronger for the breaking.'

Watson felt powerless in the face of such sorrow. 'Please forgive me,' he said. 'I can imagine how painful his loss must be.'

'My father was loved by his patients. His successor, Dr Richter, has upset a lot of people.'

Finding this a curious statement, and wondering if it might have any relevance to their enquiries — enquiries Watson had to confess that he had abandoned for time spent with this woman — he decided to probe further. 'Has he indeed? In what way — '

Before he could finish the question, however, a figure leapt out of the undergrowth onto the path before them, and Caroline screamed. Instinctively Watson moved to put himself between her and whatever had chosen that particular moment to attack them. Part of him thought it might be Holmes's mysterious limping killer, but the greater part hoped it would be Boris, returning home after adventures further afield.

It was neither. It was —

'Georg!' cried Caroline.

Ignoring her, the youngest of the Frankenstein sons fixed his burning gaze on Watson. 'We meet again,' he said in a low voice, 'and so soon!'

Caroline stepped forward. 'Georg! If you wish to speak to Dr Watson, you will address him with the respect he deserves.'

But Georg was busily parading like a young peacock in front of Watson. 'I was under the impression that you had left us, sir,' he said.

'That was my intention,' replied Watson, 'until I had the great pleasure to run into Fräulein Hertz.'

'And then what?' asked Georg. 'You sought to foist yourself upon her? At a time when grief has made her vulnerable?'

Caroline snorted. 'How dare you take that tone with — '

'Hush!' he spat. 'Can't you see this man has had designs on you from the first moment he saw you? How dare he accompany you like this with neither a guardian nor a chaperone present?'

'Georg,' Watson said with an anger he found hard to disguise, 'I realize I am a guest in your home, but that does not give you the right to impugn my good character, and it most certainly does not allow you to take such a tone with Fräulein Hertz. I will ask you to apologize, sir.'

'Apologize!' he repeated, as if the very idea were laughable. 'Not only do I refuse to apologize, Herr Doctor, but I demand satisfaction!'

Watson couldn't help it; he actually laughed. 'What?'

'Given the circumstances,' said Georg, his own expression deadly serious, 'for daring to tarnish the good name of Frankenstein, I can do no less than challenge you to a duel, Herr Doctor.'

'Georg,' said Caroline, 'you're making yourself look ridiculous!'

'On the contrary; I am defending your honour against one who would taint it,' he replied without taking his eyes off Watson. 'Herr Doctor, you will insult me if you refuse to meet me in the field.'

'Then insult you I must,' Watson replied.

'And be seen for the coward you are?'

Watson flushed from his neck up. 'Where you see cowardice, young man, I see only good common sense.'

'Then it appears I win by forfeit.'

Still upset by his earlier disagreement with Holmes, Watson's mouth tightened, the urge to teach this young jackanapes a lesson suddenly strong within him. 'It is a hollow victory, I assure you,' he said coldly. 'However . . . '

Caroline frowned at him. 'John, don't humour him.'

But Watson ignored her as an idea formed in his mind. 'Very well, Georg, I accept your challenge.'

Georg smiled thinly. 'Then we shall meet by the junction with the Mühltal road at, say, four o'clock,' he said.

'I will be there,' Watson replied calmly. Inside, however, he was wondering just what in heaven's name he'd let himself in for, and what Holmes would say about it when he found out.

'You will bring a second?' said Georg.

'I see no reason for a second,' Watson replied. 'We are both men of our word. Let us simply agree to duel until good sense prevails.'

'John!' Caroline exclaimed.

'As you wish,' said Georg.

At last Watson turned back to Caroline. 'Fräulein Hertz — ' he began.

But she shook her head to dismiss his attempted apology. 'Just go,' she advised, seeming as disappointed in him as she was angry with Georg.

'Very well,' he said stiffly. 'But I want you to know how much I regret that this had to happen.'

'As do I,' she said, clearly upset. 'I had always thought the British had more good sense than we Germans. I see now I was mistaken.'

★　★　★

Holmes retraced his steps back to Darmstadt in a thoughtful mood. Watson was his only friend, and it troubled him that they had parted on such icy terms. And yet, try as he might, he simply could not understand the appeal of the so-called fairer sex, especially when there were still riddles to be unpicked.

He was just approaching the Klein Hotel when a small, dapper man in the dark blue serge and brass-buttoned uniform of the local constabulary came out of the building and, seeing him, approached hurriedly. This was Oberwachtmeister Reiniger, whom he had met the previous night, when the senior constable — and Darmstadt's sole representative of law and order — had arrived to arrest Trautmann and his friends on the charge of attempted murder.

'Ah, Herr Holmes!' he said when he was close enough. 'You are just the man I had come to see.'

Reiniger looked as immaculate as he had the night before. His face was pale and well crafted, with gentle blue eyes and a small, typically Teutonic moustache with waxed ends.

'Am I, indeed?'

Nodding, Reiniger smiled a particularly nasty smile. 'The thought of standing trial for attempted murder has scared the wits out of Trautmann and his cronies,' he explained with relish. 'So much so that they've agreed to confess to what they see as a lesser crime, if we show leniency.'

'What is the crime?' asked Holmes.

'They confessed to stealing medical supplies from the hospital.'

Holmes's gaze immediately sharpened. 'Did they say for whom they acted?'

'Only that they were hired by a man who gave them very precise instructions, and then collected the equipment at a specified meeting point and took it away.'

'Did they describe him?'

'After a fashion. Apparently he wore a

cloak and hood and only ever met them at night, when he could hide himself in shadow.'

'His height, then? And build?'

'According to Trautmann, he was of average height, perhaps of stocky build. All three of them were vague, at best, when it came to a description.'

'Do you believe them, Oberwachtmeister?'

Reiniger replied with a definite nod. 'I do. I pride myself on being a fair judge of character, and those three were desperate to give me as much information as they could, so long as it saved them from having to face the more serious charge.'

'Well, press them a little harder. I have a feeling they may also own up to stealing from the Technical University.'

'I'll do that,' said Reiniger. Giving Holmes a sidelong look, he added, 'Does any of this help you, Herr Holmes?'

'I believe it does.'

'Thank goodness for that. We can't hush this business up indefinitely, you know.'

'I am well aware of that, Oberwacht-meister, and I am doing all in my power to bring the matter to a swift — and discreet — conclusion. Now if you will excuse me, I have another matter to attend to.'

'Of course, sir,' said Reiniger, but he hesitated, then asked, 'Anything I may be able to help you with?'

Holmes shook his head. 'No,' he replied, his thoughts already elsewhere. 'What I have in mind just now is more what you might call . . . a mission of mercy.'

11

The Blind Musician

After dismissing Liebl for what remained of the day, Watson arrived back at the inn to find Christina cleaning tables, with one stray wisp of flaxen hair hanging down the side of her pale, trouble-worn face. Of her father there was no sign.

He cleared his throat. 'Excuse me, uh . . . Christina? Do you happen to know if Herr Holmes has returned yet?'

She looked up at him, her expression as sad as ever, and shook her head in response to his question.

Realizing that he was never going to get a better chance, he said impulsively, 'Is there anything wrong that you think I could help you with? Would you like — '

Abruptly Klein rose up from behind the bar, where he had just been fetching bottles from the cellar. 'She answered your question,' he snapped. 'Your friend is not here.'

Watson turned to face him, again wanting to say more than he actually did. 'Thank you.'

He went up to his room, stripped down to his shirtsleeves and poured cold water into the bone-china basin. He washed his face, hoping to chase away some of the weariness that had claimed him, then re-dressed, checked his watch and went back downstairs.

'I wonder if you can supply me with some directions, Herr Klein?'

Klein shrugged. 'Where do you want to go?'

'The junction by the Mühltal road.'

The innkeeper made a careless gesture. 'About a mile that way, just the other side of town. But there's nothing much there, just the crossroads.'

'Thank you,' Watson replied. 'Oh, and if you see Herr Holmes, would you please tell him that I have had to go out again; that with any luck I shall see him later . . . and that I hope we are still on speaking terms?'

Klein inclined one beefy shoulder. 'I'll try,' he replied.

★ ★ ★

Watson limped through town with his hands stuffed deep into his overcoat pockets. A light mist began to fall from the leaden sky, tiny droplets bursting against skin that was already chilled enough as it was. Around him, Darmstadt was silent, its streets all but deserted. The days were short at this time of year, and the sky was already darkening with the coming of evening. And as he was starting to learn, the locals seldom ventured out after the sun went down.

Glancing up at the sky, Watson wondered if he could prevail upon Georg to postpone the duel. His hope was that, in the light of a new day, the boy would realize how foolish he had been. And yet Watson knew Georg would not be deprived of his moment of glory, especially if he stood to impress Caroline with his mis-guided attempt at chivalry.

At last the town fell behind him, and up ahead in the lonely gloom he saw the caped figure of a man standing beside a horse, waiting for him.

'I was starting to think you wouldn't come,' said Georg by way of greeting.

'I considered that option,' Watson replied, halting before him with vapour accompanying his every word. 'This whole business is ridiculous. But I gave my word.'

'Then I stand corrected,' said Georg. 'You're not a coward, after all.' He turned to the waiting horse, rummaged in a saddlebag, then brought out a polished mahogany case. Turning back to Watson, he opened the lid, revealing a matched pair of engraved and gilded French dueling pistols. As he did so, his long fingers trembled ever so slightly, betraying a fear he had thus far managed to hide.

Watson frowned. 'I thought that as the challenged party, I would have the choice of weapons.'

'I assume these will be sufficient.'

'No, sir, they will not,' said Watson. 'As the challenger, you will allow me the choice.'

Georg bit off an impulsive reply and said instead, 'Very well.'

'Then I choose,' said Watson, 'the humble word.'

Confusion crossed Georg's aristocratic face. 'What? What the devil — ?'

Watson quickly closed the distance between them. 'I agreed to duel until common sense prevailed,' he said, 'and the only way common sense will ever prevail with you is by some good old-fashioned straight talking.'

'How dare you — '

'Listen to me, Georg,' he went on, his tone urgent and earnest. 'You are a boy who is trying desperately to be a man, and in itself there is nothing wrong with that. But being a man is more than just swagger and bluster. Being a man — a man worth the name — isn't about bullying others. It's about listening; about not being afraid to admit when you're wrong; about compassion and treating those around you as you yourself would be treated. It's not about power and privilege; it's about fairness, humanity, humility.' He shook his head in sudden frustration. 'Georg ... you have the makings of a fine young man, but at the moment you're still a boy. I suggest that you enjoy your adolescence, and don't be in such a hurry to grow up.'

Georg had about him the appearance of a man who had been slapped. 'When I need your advice, Herr Doctor, I'll request it.'

'No,' said Watson. 'If you're even half as clever as you think you are, you'll take it, and think about it. What you do with it after that will determine whether or not you really can call yourself a man.'

The boy drew himself up. 'Do you know who you're talking to?'

Watson saw the anger in his eyes, and echoing what Holmes had told him earlier, said, 'The truth is a wonderful thing, Georg — but sometimes it hurts.'

'Pah! What do you know about it? You, with all your supposed wisdom?'

'I make no claims for wisdom. I hope always to learn from experience as I go along. And do you know something, Georg? I am still learning, even now, and I pray to God that I never stop. We are none of us perfect. But life is a great teacher — if we are wise enough to heed its lessons.'

He glanced back toward Darmstadt,

which was growing increasingly indistinct in the spreading twilight. 'Suppose we had fought with more than just words,' he said. 'Suppose you had wounded me — killed me, even, or vice versa. Would that have made the victor any more of a man, or his point of view any more valid than that of the man he had just wounded or worse? As hard as life can sometimes be, or seem to be . . . I love it too much to squander it. Better to judge our actions than act upon impulse.'

Georg turned and angrily stuffed the case back into his saddlebag. 'You have humiliated me, Herr Doctor,' he said bitterly.

Watson put a hand on his shoulder. Georg flinched, but didn't shrug it off. 'I didn't agree to your duel so that I could humiliate you,' he replied. 'In any case, who is here to see your supposed humiliation? I came because, in my own way, I wanted to show you that there's a better and more positive way to live; that you should enjoy your adolescence, and not ruin it by trying to be older than your years. Believe me, you'll become a man soon enough, and then there'll be plenty of times when you yearn for youth and its simplicity.' He squared his shoulders and offered his hand. 'Now,' he said, 'before we part, I would consider it a privilege to shake your hand.'

It was, of course, a test. If Georg intended to take anything away from their encounter, he would accept. If he remained as stubborn and intractable as Watson feared, he would refuse.

Georg looked up at him. 'What happened here today,' he said softly. 'It goes no further?'

'You have my word on it,' Watson assured him.

Georg himself looked off into the darkness. 'It's hard, you know, being the second son.'

'It is as hard as you choose to make it,' Watson replied. 'Now, my arm is beginning to tire. Will you shake with me or not?'

Still the boy hesitated. Then he took Watson's hand. 'I cannot promise to be the paragon of virtue you describe,' he said, and all at once he seemed even younger than he was. 'But I can try.'

'If it counts for anything,' said Watson, 'you've already gone up in my estimation.' He smiled, as much with relief as anything else. 'Now, go on back to the castle, and make your peace with Clemens and Caroline.'

★ ★ ★

As night fell, Clemens felt an all-too-familiar restlessness build within him. He knew also that there was nothing he could do to stop it.

He was well aware that he possessed an overly sensitive nature, of course; but he was an artist, and that was to be expected. Still . . . sometimes the very sensitivity of his soul was itself a curse. To find pain in the way the sun sometimes set, or to play a melody so beautiful that it made him weep not with joy but with the frustration of knowing that he himself would never compose anything so heartfelt . . . And yet he could no more change the way he was inside than he could change the colour of his eyes. And so he had to live with the awfulness of simply being himself.

No one knew how heavy that burden was to bear. How could they? Sometimes, and more often these days, he found himself looking at those around him and wondering how they could be so . . . so *normal*. Clemens doubted that he could be normal even if his life depended on it; and sometimes he felt that, if not his life, then certainly his very sanity did.

For as long as he could remember, he'd had an unshakable conviction that bad things always happened at night. He'd tried to conquer this fear by taking long midnight walks, as he was doing just now. By deliberately making his way to the darkest, remotest sections of the surrounding woods, he hoped always to prove his misgivings unfounded.

And yet still they persisted. He suspected they always would.

Suddenly he froze in mid-stride and his head jerked, bird-like, toward the inky darkness off to his left. He listened, but all around him the woods were silent. And yet he had been sure . . .

Then — there it was again! Incredibly, amazingly, someone was playing a violin out there!

He could hardly believe it, and for one brief moment he felt sure he must be going mad. But when he strained his ears he could actually identify the piece being played. It was by Wagner: 'Geliebter, komm! Sieh dort die Grotte' from *Tannhäuser*.

Excited beyond belief, he threw his customary caution to the wind and immediately began to blunder through the forest toward the music. He was mad, he knew it; but to find someone else in this lifeless place who could play so exquisitely and express his clear love for music was something he could not resist.

Suddenly the music stopped.

He slowed to a halt, his spirits sinking. Perhaps it had been his imagination after all. Perhaps he had only heard what he'd wanted to hear —

But then he heard it again, drifting in from the darkness; and following the sound, he hurried on around trees and bushes, over deadfalls and carpets of fallen leaves. The woods enveloped him completely. Night creatures flew or shuffled away in the darkness before him. Then, abruptly, the music stopped again, and so did Clemens.

He waited and listened. Nothing but silence.

Until the sweet strains of Wagner came again . . . and once again lured him on.

For fully five minutes, Clemens blundered through the darkness, until he realized that the music was leading him toward a small fire that was just visible through the screening undergrowth. Bushes rustled and branches cracked as he fought his way ever closer to the little clearing in which a tall man in rags stood playing the violin.

Warily, Clemens studied him from a distance. He had never seen the fellow before. He wore a wide-brimmed hat from beneath which wispy white hair hung to his shoulders. His torn-and-never-repaired coat and old ankle-jack boots reinforced the idea that he was a tramp. But never had a common vagabond been able to coax a sweeter melody from any instrument.

174

He went closer, his foot accidentally coming down on a fallen twig and snapping it noisily. The tramp immediately stopped playing and turned; his chin, from which trailed a long, wispy grey beard, held high. 'Who's there?' he called in a weak, quavering voice. 'Who are you?'

For a moment Clemens debated the wisdom of going nearer. But he had come this far. And though he suddenly felt quite foolish about it, he was intrigued by this man who had elected to camp illegally on Frankenstein land.

'It's all right,' he called. 'I mean you no harm. I . . . I heard you playing, is all.'

'A music lover,' said the old man, and as Clemens came closer he saw with surprise that the man was blind. Set either side of a long nose purpled by broken veins, the old man's milky white eyes stared out into his own personal darkness. 'Please . . . come closer. If truth be told, I welcome the company. Do you play yourself?'

'I . . . yes, I do.'

The blind man offered his violin, a

battered old piece. 'Would you care to play something now? For me?'

'I don't — '

'Please. I should like to hear you.'

Clemens felt strangely, absurdly pleased by the request. He took the violin from the other man's grimy fingers and tucked it under his chin, settled the bow on the strings, positioned his fingers . . . and then began to play, his bandaged hand showing no signs of impairing his performance.

'The 'Violin Sonata in E',' the blind man cackled, 'by Richard Strauss. You have talent, sir.'

Clemens stopped playing. 'So they say.'

'You are a student of music, I presume?'

'Yes, I wish to . . . well, I would have liked to embrace a musical career.'

The old man frowned as the shadows cast by the small fire danced across his face. 'Did you give up?'

'I'm still undecided,' Clemens confessed. 'My family supports me, but I am the eldest son, and so I should probably follow after my father. You know, take on

176

his rank and status.'

The old man appeared to consider that for a long moment. At length he asked, 'Did he tell you that was his wish?'

'He would never do that. But I don't want to disappoint him. I would rather give up music, at least for a little while.'

'You are local, sir?'

'I am Clemens von Frankenstein.'

The blind man licked his lips nervously. 'I think I am on your land,' he said. 'I am sorry, *meine Herr*. I'll — '

'You're not in anyone's way,' said Clemens. 'And you have a nice, cosy little camp here. I see no reason why you shouldn't stay as long as you like.'

'Do . . . do you mean that, sir?'

'Of course.'

'Why, th-thank you.'

Looking closer at the few meagre possessions this vagabond owned, and realizing just how privileged he himself had always been, Clemens said impulsively, 'The dog at the house barks at me every time I play, so I said he bit me to the bone.'

The tramp stared at him through his

sightless eyes. 'And did he?' he asked softly.

Clemens's face clouded instantly. 'No. I simply cut my palm with a razor blade to make it look as if he had. And now I feel dreadful about it — especially since the dog has vanished. Childish, isn't it?'

'Not at all.'

'I don't even know why I'm telling you all this.'

The old tramp shrugged. 'We all need someone to talk to sometimes. And sometimes it's easier to talk to strangers we'll never see again.' He made another gesture. 'Let me hear you play again. You really do know your instrument, you know.'

'Do you think so?'

'I do. And I think it would be a crime if you chose not to pursue the gift you have been given.'

'You make it sound as if I have a choice.'

'Every man has a choice,' said the old tramp. 'Yours is to follow your heart and pursue that which gives you joy, or to spend the rest of your days as the most miserable baron the Frankensteins have ever known.'

Clemens laughed bitterly. 'Either way, I bring shame to the family name.'

'No,' said the blind man. 'Because it so happens there is a third choice.'

Clemens eyed him curiously. 'Which is . . . ?'

'To combine the two,' came the simple reply. 'To be the baron, and carry out all the duties that such a position entails, and in the quieter moments that must inevitably come, go off and travel the world, pursuing your love of music and performance. It can be done, you know. One does not necessarily preclude the other.'

Clemens looked at him for a long moment, and it was as if a weight had been lifted from him. The only sound was the low crackling of the campfire, until at length he cleared his throat. 'Thank you,' he said sincerely. 'For a blind man, you have helped me to see things much more clearly.'

And with much to think about, he returned the violin to the vagabond and began to make his way back to the castle.

12

Leave Her to Me

Watson woke with a start, though he was not entirely sure why. He must have dozed off at some point. Now the room was in darkness. He listened for a while but heard nothing. Then a door slammed somewhere on the floor above, and footsteps clattered hurriedly, almost angrily, downstairs. There came a muffled exchange of words from below, but aside from the fact that they were the voices of men, he could make out nothing more.

He wondered if he should find out what was going on. Then there came the slam of another door, and . . . silence.

⋆   ⋆   ⋆

As the inn fell behind him, Dr Richter felt his fury mounting, along with the pain in his face, where Christina had scratched him.

180

How dare she? Who did the little trollop think she was, anyway? Klein had assured him that the girl would be a compliant, if not entirely willing, partner in his evening's ... entertainment. Instead, she had fought him with an intensity that bordered on desperation, finally raking his face and drawing blood. The bitch!

Around him, Darmstadt was safely tucked in for the night. That was a mercy — it meant there had been no one around to witness his humiliation. He stopped in a side street and used his handkerchief to mop the tiny beads of blood that marked the passage of her nails.

Of course, he had repaid her for that. A hard slap had sent the half-naked woman reeling across her miserable little room. He had shouted an obscenity at her, too. But that had been a mistake; it might well have drawn the attention of the *Engländer* who were staying at the inn. Still, with the oath yelled, he had gathered his coat and stormed downstairs, there to confront Klein.

He allowed himself a cold smile at the

recollection of that encounter. He had offered the innkeeper his usual stack of coins, only to snatch them away the minute Klein had reached for them. There would be no payment for the one-legged man this night.

'You assured me that your daughter would not be opposed to a bit of . . . originality,' Richter had grated between clenched teeth.

Klein shrugged. 'Maybe she didn't understand. She's not used to it.'

'She'd better be more amenable next time, Klein, or we'll see how you get on without my custom!'

'Leave her to me,' Klein had said.

But by then Richter was stepping out into the night and slamming the door behind him, the anger that had been simmering in him for the past several days finally approaching boiling point.

* * *

For a moment Klein just looked at the door. Richter was right, damn him. He paid well for the privilege of indulging his warped desires with Christina — for that, and Klein's silence about it. Klein would hate to lose that extra money. And he was damned if he would.

Slowly his expression on his pocked face hardened. He limped out from behind the counter and went, very slowly, upstairs to his daughter's bedroom. He entered without knocking and found Christina sitting on the edge of her bed. Her head snapped around when he entered, her hands flying from her face, where tears still shone in her eyes.

'Get up,' he said softly.

She looked at him, her frown asking the question.

'Get up, and get out,' he said harshly.

Still she looked at him, her expression mingling horror with confusion now.

'Get up and get out!' he said again, his patience wearing thin. 'You've caused me to lose face with Richter! Maybe you'll think twice before you do that again, after spending the night outside!'

When she still didn't move, he lunged forward, grabbed her by one arm and dragged her from the room. It was all she could do not to tumble down the stairs as he yanked her across the floor and threw her roughly out into the night. Before she even properly knew what had happened, he'd slammed the door behind her.

Christina stood there for a moment, not really knowing what to do next. After a few seconds the lamps inside the inn were extinguished and the windows went dark. Shivering, she turned and wandered away, hugging herself against the cold. Low to begin with, the temperature now dropped like a stone, and she knew she'd be lucky to survive the night if she didn't find shelter quickly. But shelter where? Her father was not widely liked in Darmstadt, and consequently she had never found it easy to make friends for herself. The simple truth was that there was no one else who might offer shelter, a fact he knew all too well.

There was, however, a stable behind the inn. It wasn't much, but she could make it as warm and comfortable as she could, and it was better than nothing. She hurried towards it, the cobbles ice-cold against her bare feet. She entered the stable and considered lighting the closed lantern hanging beside the door so that she could see to make herself a bed in the hay, but decided against it. She didn't want to risk her father seeing the light and coming to throw her out into the night all over again.

The stable was empty. She had her pick of the stalls, and felt she could make herself warm and comfortable enough to survive the night. Perhaps in the morning her father would have calmed down. Perhaps he might even see that it wasn't right, what he had allowed the doctor to do to her. But she didn't hold out much hope there. Her father had always been a cold man, even more so after Christina's mother had left him. It was almost as if he had punished Christina for what happened, because her mother was no longer there to be a target for his hatred.

Then all thought was suddenly wiped clean from her mind, and she turned, knowing without knowing why that she was not alone in the hay-smelling darkness. As if to confirm it, a figure stepped out of the shadows to stand silhouetted in the stable door. A tall man with broad shoulders.

'Well, well,' said Dr Richter, and she drew in a startled breath when she recognized his voice. 'Look who it is. The bitch who thinks she's too good for me!'

★ ★ ★

Watson had just convinced himself that he was reading too much into a few innocuous sounds — the slamming of doors, the sounds of footsteps descending the stairs, a conversation between two men — when he heard what he felt sure was a scream.

He struggled up from his bed, his first thought for Christina, who had started to dominate his thoughts almost as much as Caroline Hertz. He was halfway to the door when he heard footsteps clattering urgently against the cobbles below. Changing direction, he hurried to the window and was just in time to see what appeared to be a woman in a nightdress racing toward the nearby forest, and a large man in pursuit of her. The woman's long, pale yellow hair identified her as Christina Klein, but the light was too poor to identify her pursuer.

Not stopping to think, although he was most certainly aware that the woman who couldn't — or wouldn't — speak had now found her voice, he snatched up his suit jacket and tore open the door. Ignoring his old leg wound, he made it to the ground floor in record time. The lobby was dark and empty, and he collided with a table and some chairs before he made it to the door. Cursing, he fumbled with the bolt and a moment later was out in the courtyard, the breath misting before his face.

Pausing only to tear his Webley from his pocket, he set off into the woods. He could see practically nothing, and all he could hear were the sounds of his own clumsy blunderings as he hurried ever deeper into the darkness. He stopped, straining his ears. His breathing was harsh, but try as he might, he was unable to quieten it.

Blast it, where had Christina and her pursuer gone?

As if in answer, she suddenly screamed again; and if ever a sound could truly chill the blood, that was it. Clasping his revolver even tighter, Watson ran on in the direction of the cry.

The woods swallowed him up. Undaunted, he ran on. Then, without warning, he collided with someone coming from the opposite direction. They bounced off each other and stumbled to the ground. Watson stared at the man, but it was too dark to make out anything other than a vague impression — that he was hatless, and that the moonlight shone on what appeared to be short, fair hair.

Then the man was back on his feet and running as fast as he could back in the direction of the town, and before Watson could think more about it, there came another soul-chilling scream. Dismissing the man from his mind, though he had almost certainly been Christina's pursuer, he once more set off in the direction of the terrified woman. Up ahead there seemed to be a clearing of some sort. Moonlight shafted down into the grassy bowl, to show him —

The woman screamed again.

A man — no, a *giant* — was standing before her, the tails of his soiled trench coat swinging around his calves.

Watson stopped, utterly stupefied by the sight before him. The giant was a deformed monstrosity of a man dressed in tattered rags, with a soiled bandage wound around his head . . . but a head that appeared massively and grotesquely out of proportion on one side. It raised long arms towards Christina that ended in clawed hands the size of dinner plates, and with one final scream she collapsed before him.

Watson burst into the clearing, immediately trying to put himself between the . . . the *thing* and the unconscious girl. The monster — for that was surely what it was — had the moon behind it, so the bulk of it was still in shadow. But seeing him, it grunted something unintelligible.

Watson raised the pistol and cried, 'Stay back! Stay back, or so help me I will fire!'

He had no idea whether or not the creature understood him. It was impossible to read anything into its low, raspy grunts. But the next moment it sprang at him, and with a flinch he pulled the trigger. The Webley barked and twitched in his hand, and the thing hunched up with a snarl of pain.

And then . . . it kept coming.

Hardly able to believe it, Watson's eyes widened as its shadow fell across him. Then it lashed out, swatting him as if he were nothing more bothersome than a wasp. He tumbled sideways and slammed hard against the bole of a tree. For a fleeting moment he threatened to lose consciousness, but somehow fought against it because he knew that if he didn't, Christina's fate was most assuredly sealed.

Now the monster reached down and lifted Christina easily into his arms. Revived by the movement, she stirred back to life and a second later screamed again, as she saw the thing that held her captive.

Stumbling to his feet, Watson threw himself at the creature's broad back, knowing even as he did so that he stood no more chance of stopping it with his fists than he had with his revolver. The giant stiffened at his blows, but not with pain; only annoyance. And then, holding Christina firmly in one massive arm, he used the other to bat Watson aside.

Again he flew across the clearing and smashed to the earth with a force that woke pain in every limb. The world tilted madly before him. He knew he was going to pass out this time; knew also that there was nothing he could do to stop it. And as his vision blurred he saw the . . . the thing . . . lumbering toward him with Christina still screaming in its arms, and knew that this was the last thing he would ever see.

He closed his eyes, hating the fact that he had let Christina down; that she now faced a fate far worse than anything he could imagine, and there was nothing he could do to save her. He felt the ground tremble underfoot with every ponderous, crunching step the creature took towards him. He heard the deep rumbling of its every slow breath as it came closer; the low growl that accompanied every fetid exhalation. His ears were filled with a high-pitched whistling sound, and he knew that this was the end. Fighting to open his eyes and failing miserably, he set his teeth and waited for the inevitable. The whistling seemed to reach a crescendo, and then . . .

He heard the footsteps turn and slowly, slowly recede.

The thing was sparing him!

And it was with that incredulous thought in mind that Watson finally surrendered to unconsciousness.

★ ★ ★

He would have been quite happy to stay cosseted in the darkness, but it seemed that someone else had other ideas. That someone kept slapping insistently at his face.

'Watson! Watson, are you all right?'

He opened his eyes, expecting to see Holmes — for it was Holmes's voice that he recognized — but crouched over him instead was an old man with a wide-brimmed hat and a long wispy beard.

'What — ?' he managed, trying to struggle up. 'Who the devil — ?'

His rescuer tore off his beard and threw back the disreputable old hat, and at once the blind tramp who had made such an impression on Clemens von Frankenstein came more to resemble Holmes.

'What happened?' Holmes persisted.

Watson sat up slowly, checking himself for broken ribs. 'Christina!' he breathed. 'She was taken by that . . . monster from hell! Go after them!'

Holmes hesitated momentarily, torn between remaining with his injured friend and following the logical course Watson had dictated. Logic won, and with a nod he straightened to his full height, and with his old tramp's coat billowing around him, turned and went in pursuit of whatever had abducted Christina.

Watson watched him vanish into the mist, and was not aware that he had passed out again until he opened his eyes to see Holmes striding back toward him. Fighting back to a sitting position, he said, 'Don't tell me you lost their trail?'

'That is precisely what I did, confound the luck!'

'Then you . . . you didn't see it?'

Holmes regarded him grimly. 'I didn't have to. I saw its tracks . . . tracks that spoke of something large and heavy and yet . . . human.' He fell silent for a moment, as if he had surprised himself with the statement. Then: 'Tell me everything that happened to you. Omit nothing, no matter how seemingly trivial.'

Watson ordered his thoughts and then recounted the events of the evening. When he was finished, Holmes's eyes were aglow. 'Your account of tonight's events casts a new light on this whole business,' he assured his friend. 'Come, let us get you back to the inn. You have had a very narrow escape, and will need rest before we proceed.'

'No,' said Watson, retrieving his revolver. 'We have to find Christina — '

'There is little we can do for her at the moment, hampered as we are by the darkness. But at first light I promise we will do everything in our power to find her, and hopefully save her.'

'But what are we saving her from, exactly? Holmes, that . . . that *thing* was a giant! Surely no man born of woman could grow to such a size!'

'I do not believe it *was* born of woman.'

'What?'

'I have no further doubts about this, Watson. The fictitious Victor Frankenstein has an imitator here.'

Watson's immediate response was a heartfelt: 'Impossible!' But then he remembered the thing that had abducted Christina, and added with rather less conviction, 'Isn't it?'

'One element of your story has me particularly intrigued,' Holmes responded as they made their way back through the forest. 'Why would the creature's skull be so deformed?'

'It cannot possibly be out of aesthetic considerations.'

'Of course not. But there has to be a reason, Watson! No scientist would bother to complicate an experiment without a reason.'

Watson suggested irritably, 'Maybe to have it wear two hats?'

To his surprise, Holmes's face lit up. 'Watson, you are brilliant!'

'Really, Holmes, you believe that two hats — '

'Not hats, Watson, but rather . . . two brains!'

Watson stopped dead in his tracks. 'Two b — In God's name, two brains for a single head?'

'Indeed. And it would explain . . . '

'What?'

'I need to clarify a few points before I say more, but I hope to clear the mist surrounding this case very soon now.'

13

The Scent of Death

Clemens retired to bed that night, by turns elated and troubled. The meeting with the blind man had been a revelation to him. In the end, it had been so easy to open up and talk frankly about the things that had haunted him for so long. And the blind man's simple advice had struck deep within him — *Every man has a choice. Yours is to follow your heart and pursue that which gives you joy, or to spend the rest of your days as the most miserable baron the Frankensteins have ever known.*

He had gone straight home, pausing only once when he thought he heard a gunshot in the distance, and found his family in the drawing room. Girding himself, he had stood before them and confessed two things: that he had wounded himself in the hope of somehow discrediting Caroline's beloved Boris, and that he did not wish to inherit the Frankenstein estate unless, in turn, he could also pursue his first and only love — music.

He had braced himself for the expected explosion, but in the event it failed to materialise. Even Georg had resisted the urge to condemn him. Instead, and to his eternal gratitude, his father had given his confession long, quiet consideration, then said gently, 'Clemens, I know that the prospect of one day becoming the new baron has been a source of great concern to you. I would be blind not to see where your true love lies, and I would hate to see you trapped in a place or a position that makes you unhappy. Therefore, if music really is your life, then what sort of a father would I be to stop you from embracing it?'

'I *will* embrace it, father,' Clemens replied in a voice thick with emotion. 'But I will embrace my role as baron as well, when the time comes. I swear to you I will be the best I can be. And when time and duty permit, I will also have a life beyond the confines of this castle, of Darmstadt, and of Germany itself. It may be difficult to balance the two, but I will do it, and I will never see shame brought to our family name. Upon that I give you my solemn word.'

Impulsively the baron rose and took his son's hand. The shake was warm and filled with emotion. To Clemens's amazement, Georg had also stepped forward to shake his hand. Clemens hesitated briefly, sure that there must be some other motive behind his brother's action, but no; when at last he took the hand, Georg's shake was firm and sincere.

'Anything I can do to help,' said Georg, 'you have only to ask.'

Clemens was speechless. But when he looked Georg in the eye, he saw that his brother meant it. 'Thank you,' he replied; and then, impulsively, they hugged each other.

Georg knew a moment of pleasure he had never thought possible. Earlier, when he had apologized to Caroline for his earlier actions, the look on her face had been a wonderful reward. He had seen the surprise there, of course, and a hint of doubt, as if he couldn't possibly mean what he had just said. But then into her eyes had come a warmth and respect he had thought never to see there, and he knew that the *Engländer*, Watson, had been right. There was time enough to grow up.

But then the mood in the room seemed to change somehow, and Baron Frankenstein looked at each of them in turn with clear discomfort. 'Coming to me about your little . . . hoax,' he said, gesturing to his son's bandaged hand, 'was a courageous act. Your frankness honours you, but in a way it puts me to shame.'

Clemens and Georg exchanged a puzzled look.

'You see, I also have a secret to share,' the Baron explained heavily.

And what followed tempered the joy Clemens and Georg had just found. Indeed, it shattered it.

★ ★ ★

Much later, still sequestered in the drawing room, the baron stared into the dying embers of the fire and wondered if he had done the right thing. Caroline and his sons had a right to know, of course. And yet, unburdening himself as he had only left him feeling even more troubled.

Suddenly restless, he stood up and went to the night-black window. His reflection stared back at him like some grim, transparent doppelganger. It was well past midnight, but he knew there would be no rest for him this night. All at once the room seemed stuffy and confining, and on impulse he decided to go outside into the bracing night air.

The night was freezing, the star-spattered sky clear and seemingly boundless. Pausing on the steps before the great house, he looked up at the heavens and shivered. After a time he wandered thoughtfully toward the gardens at the side of the house. The scents of winter-flowering honeysuckle, gold-edged daphne and chartreuse-coloured copse laurel had a calming effect upon him and, as he had hoped it would, helped him get his problems into perspective. That was, until the scents of the flowers were replaced by the smells of peat, or burnt earth, or aged whiskey.

Then he realized with a start that someone was standing on the path some yards ahead of him. He thought at first that it might be Georg or Clemens, and that the impression of tremendous size was just a trick of the darkness. But now the smell was overpowering.

'Who . . . who's there?' he asked.

The figure — a huge man in a long trench coat, his bandaged head seeming somehow lopsided and all the more grotesque because of it — made a peculiar rasping sound that was almost impossible to decipher.

'Who *are* you?' asked the baron, struggling to keep the alarm out of his voice.

'Don't . . . you . . . know?' asked the giant in a voice that sounded more like pebbles trickling across broken glass. 'Can't . . . you . . . guess?'

The baron didn't have a chance to even consider an answer, for the giant started limping toward him even before the last word had left what passed for his lips. The baron turned and broke into a panicky run back to the courtyard — but before he could cover more than a few yards, thick fingers clamped him by the shoulders and lifted him off his feet. He hung suspended in the air, legs kicking desperately until the giant released his grip on one shoulder and, using that free hand, slapped him hard across the side of the head.

The baron fell unconscious.

* * *

In Darmstadt, Johann Klein took the news of his daughter's abduction harder than he had thought possible.

'She . . . she was taken?' he asked again, his voice low, his tone one of absolute bafflement.

'I am afraid so,' Holmes replied. 'By something that was able to withstand the impact of a bullet fired at near point-blank range, and was possessed of quite prodigious strength.'

'Who — ?'

'The question just now is why she was out on so bitter a night in nothing more than a nightdress.'

'I . . . don't know,' said the innkeeper.

'Come now,' snapped Holmes. 'It is highly unlikely that you would be unaware that your daughter had left the premises. Dr Watson here has already told me he heard raised voices — those of a man or men, one of whom was most probably yourself, the other a man who chased her into the forest and then apparently made himself scarce when whatever abducted your daughter appeared on the scene. Did you and she have an argument of some sort? Perhaps a disagreement over her behaviour?'

'Certainly not!'

'And yet you have, have you not, been selling the use of your daughter's body for money?'

Klein shot up from his chair, shoving it back across the floor with a loud scrape of sound. 'That is a wretched thing to say!' he said. 'You can get out, the pair of you, right now!'

But Holmes stood his ground. 'How many were there, I wonder?' he mused with a disdainful curl of the lip. 'Dr

Richter was one of them, that is certain.'

'Is it, indeed?' sneered Klein.

'Of course. I myself saw him paying you for your daughter's services last night. I imagine that is why Frau Richter left him in such a sorry state and took their daughter with her.'

Watson started. 'Left him? I thought he said his wife had gone to visit relatives in — '

'No, Watson,' Holmes replied. 'It is unlikely that she would have left her wedding ring on the corner of Richter's mantelpiece were she not intending to leave him altogether. And even allowing for the need to take their child away from Darmstadt in the wake of what she had witnessed at the cemetery, a sudden trip to Malmö — a distance of more than five hundred miles — seems somewhat excessive. It is my contention that she discovered the truth about Richter's indiscretions and left him.' He fixed his gimlet stare on the innkeeper. 'He was here again tonight, wasn't he? It was he who chased Christina into the woods, and in all probability sealed her fate.'

Klein's lips trembled, and he suddenly buried his face in his hands. 'Yes,' he sobbed wretchedly. 'Yes, it was Richter, damn him!'

Holmes stood back. 'Very well. We will see to Richter once we have concluded our present business. For now, however, we must think of Christina, and do everything in our power to rescue her.'

'If she's still anywhere to be found,' Klein whispered wretchedly.

★　★　★

Sleep was practically impossible for Watson. The best he could manage was a restless doze as he waited for dawn and the chance to search for Christina. When the first glimmer of the new day began to creep over the forested slopes and illuminate Schloss Frankenstein, perched high to the south, he heard footsteps outside his door, followed by a gentle rapping of knuckles.

He almost tore the door off its hinges in his rush to open it. Holmes stood outside, dressed for the hike they intended to make.

'Are you ready?' he asked.

Watson nodded. 'Just let me fetch my overcoat and my revolver.'

Downstairs, they found Klein still seated at one of his tables, where they had left him late the night before. The innkeeper looked ghastly. A single thought had haunted his every second: *What have I done? What have I done?*

At the sounds they made descending the stairs, he seemed to come out of his gloom and push himself upright. 'Give me a moment,' he said. 'I'm coming with you.'

Even as he said it, there came a heavy thumping at the door. Klein froze, staring at Holmes and Watson. Then: 'It's her!' he said, and amazingly, there was a catch of real emotion in his throat as he said it. He thump-walked across to the door, tore off the bar and swung the portal wide. 'Christina — ' he began — and stopped.

Helder was standing on the threshold, with Oberwachtmeister Reiniger beside him and Liebl hovering behind them. All three men looked pale in the early-morning gloom; pale and somehow numb with shock.

'Johann,' said Helder, taking the inn-keeper by the shoulder.

Klein shook his head. 'Not now, Burgomaster. We have to go out — '

'It's Christina,' said Reiniger. 'Johann . . . we have some bad news.'

'No . . . ' he said, still shaking his head. 'No . . . '

Helder steered him deeper into the room. 'I think you had better sit down.'

★ ★ ★

The news was just about as bad as it could possibly be. A local carpenter named Schneider had been out collecting wood in the hills to the south when he had found Christina's body crudely hidden in some undergrowth. Her neck had been snapped and she had been dead for some hours. But ante-mortem, it appeared that she had been sexually violated.

Klein himself heard no more. The victim of a guilty conscience, he broke down and started sobbing.

Holmes and Watson could only exchange a grim glance. The worst had happened, and Watson had to swallow hard and steel himself, for he saw now that he would never get the chance to help Christina as he had hoped, and improve what had been a truly wretched existence for her.

But there was no time just then to process all the implications of Christina's death. While Reiniger told Klein that, hard as it was, he would have to identify the body, Helder took the two *Engländer* aside.

'This is a terrible business,' he said, sotto voce. 'And Christina's death isn't the end of it.'

'What do you mean?' asked Holmes.

'I fear we have another mystery on our hands,' Helder said bleakly. 'It's the baron. He's disappeared.'

'What do you mean, disappeared?'

'Clemens sent one of the Frankenstein servants, Bohmer, into Darmstadt late last night to say that his father had just vanished. There's no sign of him anywhere.'

'Is he sure? It is a property of considerable size.'

'Apparently Clemens had the castle

turned upside down when he realized the baron was nowhere to be found. He also had the grounds checked.'

'What about Caroline?' Watson asked anxiously. 'I mean, Fräulein Hertz?'

Helder looked at him. 'She is safe enough, thank goodness.'

'Very well, Burgomaster,' said Holmes. 'We will assist in any way we can. But in one respect, I believe you are mistaken.'

'How so?' asked Helder.

'This is not another mystery, as you call it. Rather, I suspect that it is all part of the same one.'

14

The Curse of Frankenstein

Leaving the still-slumbering town behind them, Holmes and Watson made their way into the forest, following the course Christina had taken the night before while being pursued by Lars Richter. A low, cloying mist that smelled like sulphur drifted among the closely packed trees. Neither man spoke as they waded grimly through it.

After a time they reached the clearing in which Watson had had his encounter with the giant. The place looked no less grim in the growing daylight. While Watson looked around uneasily, and birds began to greet the new day with song, Holmes began a systematic, painstaking examination of the forest floor. The grass the giant had flattened beneath him last night had had plenty of time to spring back, and his footprints were no longer so easy to discern. But nothing of such size could move through the forest and not leave any sign of its passing, and soon Holmes said crisply, 'This way.'

Side by side, they worked their way deeper into the gloomy woods until fresher prints showed Holmes where the carpenter, Schneider, had discovered Christina's body.

Even though the body had long since been removed, Watson was still struck by an overwhelming sense of sadness as he studied the spot where Christina had been defiled and slaughtered. That such a sad life should come to such a sad end infuriated him with its injustice, and his failure to protect her wracked him with guilt.

As if sensing his thoughts, Holmes touched him gently on the shoulder. 'Come on,' he said softly. 'I've found more tracks.'

Up across the wooded slopes they climbed, Holmes occasionally muttering to himself. Once he said, 'Look at that stride — five feet if it's an inch!' He sank to one knee, took out a tape measure and busied himself gauging the length of the foot, the width of the heel, the depth of the prints. Though he made no further comment after that, Watson couldn't help but see the amazement and, yes, fear in his grey eyes.

Then they were off again; and though the steep ascent soon took its toll on both men, neither one considered abandoning the chase, nor of resting to regain his breath. Watson's leg wound began to act up, exacerbated as much by the dampness of the day as by the angle of the mountain; but he ignored it. At that moment it was more important to bring Christina's killer to justice.

Gradually the incline began to level out, and through the close-packed trees Watson discerned grey crenelated fieldstone walls cornered by angular towers. This was no surprise to him. He had known all along that the trail would lead to Schloss Frankenstein.

As they paused at last to catch their breath, Holmes said in a low tone, 'From here on we must proceed with even greater caution.'

At length the forest thinned and they found themselves in the shrubbery that bordered the castle gardens. The castle itself appeared silent and deserted, the fog giving everything an odd, unreal appearance, especially the topiary figures of elephants and men. But the tracks they had followed all the way from the scene of the murder were still clear to see in the dew-wet grass, stretching across the manicured lawn toward the side of the house itself.

'Come on,' hissed Holmes.

Together they crossed the lawn until they came to a trelliswork of roses at which the tracks simply ended. 'Another puzzle,' mused Holmes.

But after close examination, Watson shook his head. 'No. Look.' And parting the roses, he revealed a gap in the trellis that allowed entry to a short stone staircase that led down to a sunken door.

'Well, well, what have we here?' Descending the steps, Holmes produced his small tension wrench and bent to pick the lock. On this occasion, however, the endeavour quickly proved to be impossible. 'Blast it!'

he breathed. 'No matter. We know our prey is in the castle somewhere. All we have to do now is find him and bring him to justice. Come on!' And without another word, he set off around to the front of the house.

They were just mounting the front steps when someone yelled, 'You there! Halt!' As they turned, the manservant, Bohmer, came striding toward them from the far side of the courtyard with a heavy flintlock blunderbuss in his hands. 'You, *Engländers!*' he called. 'What are you doing here?' Watson cursed.

'We have come to see your masters,' said Holmes.

'My masters are not here,' said Bohmer, indicating the countryside beyond the castle walls with a quick flick of the head. 'They're out there somewhere, looking for the baron.'

'Then we shall wait,' Holmes insisted.

Something in Bohmer's expression changed then; hardened. Suddenly he aimed the blunderbuss right at them, and now there was nothing at all subservient in his manner. Now he appeared to stand taller and more assured.

'Put your hands up,' he said softly.

'What the deuce do you — ' Watson began.

But Holmes only smiled briefly and coldly. 'I see,' he murmured, his voice deceptively calm. 'You were the mysterious go-between, weren't you, Bohmer? The man in the shadows who arranged the purchase of the stolen medical supplies and equipment.'

Ignoring him, Bohmer barked, 'Get your hands up, I said.' When they had done as he demanded, the manservant moved in as close as he dared and patted each man down for weapons. Finding Watson's revolver, he smiled coldly and stuffed the weapon into his waistband. 'All right — now turn around and go inside.'

Holmes and Watson exchanged a look. At that moment there was nothing they could possibly do that would not result in injury or death. The large-calibre blunderbuss — an early forerunner to the shotgun — would inflict devastating wounds to both men if fired at such close range. That being the case, they turned and went up the steps, hands still raised. Bohmer followed them at a distance that kept him well out of their reach.

'Inside,' Bohmer growled again.

Holmes opened the door and they went in. The spacious lobby was filled with the echo of their footsteps. Watson looked around, trying vainly to find something he might use as a makeshift weapon to turn the tables.

'The library,' Bohmer said in a soft, tight voice. 'Come on.'

Holmes and Watson crossed to the library door. The suits of armour flanking it stared blindly ahead. Holmes twisted the handle and they went inside. Bohmer followed them in and closed the door behind him. At the manservant's command, they came to a halt in the centre of the musty room.

'Over there,' said Bohmer, with the thrust of the blunderbuss. 'Those shelves with all the copies of *Frankenstein* on them.'

Once again they did as they were told.

'You,' said Bohmer, addressing Holmes. 'Take the last three books off the third shelf down.'

Holmes turned and eyed him askance.

'Do it!' grated Bohmer.

Holmes did as he was told.

'Now reach into the gap. You'll find a lever. Turn it.'

Holmes did so, and felt around until his fingertips brushed against something long, metallic and cold to the touch. He paused only briefly, then turned the lever. A moment later he was rewarded by a click, and a door-sized opening in the bookcase swung open silently. Watson mouthed, *Good grief*.

'Inside, the pair of you.'

With another glance at each other, Holmes and Watson stepped into the darkness behind the bookcase.

★ ★ ★

Frau Vogler was arranging vases of flowers to brighten the wards of Saint Corbinian's when she heard the distinctive thump of Johann Klein's wooden peg on the tiled floor. She looked up from her chore and, recognizing Klein but not yet knowing what had happened to his

218

daughter, smiled and said, 'Herr Klein! I hope everything is — '

Then she saw that he was holding Trautmann's Mannlicher-Carcano carbine in both his large hands. 'H-Herr Klein?'

The innkeeper paid her no mind; indeed, he was so focused on the course he had set for himself that afterward the almoner doubted he'd even heard her.

She came from behind the desk and tentatively reached out a hand to stop him. But then he was gone, thump-limping down the corridor until he reached a door marked 'Doktor Lars Richter'.

He twisted the handle and shoved the door open. Richter was behind his desk, staring at a stack of medical reports and not seeing them at all. All he had seen since the previous night was the thing that had come out of nowhere and grabbed Christina; the thing he had fled from in sheer terror.

His square-jawed face snapped up as the door flew open. His blue eyes went large as he recognized Klein. His mouth fell open as he saw the innkeeper raise the carbine, and he said, 'No! W-wait!'

Then Klein pulled the trigger and the bullet punched through Richter's sternum, hurling him backwards over the chair to slam hard against the wall behind him. Richter slid down the wall, a flower of blood blooming in the centre of his chest, a worm of it spilling from his slack lips. His eyes glassed over as his life deserted him.

Watching him die, Klein felt none of the satisfaction he had expected from the sight. Behind him he heard the urgent clatter and echo of footsteps approaching at speed, a confusion of voices, and even a scream.

Then he upended the carbine, closed his lips around the still-warm barrel, and with his thumb pulled the trigger again.

★　★　★

Holmes and Watson found themselves in a narrow, dusty passageway built from rough-hewn blocks, with a low, damp-smelling ceiling. A few yards to the right there lay a claustrophobic passageway that doubtless led to the sunken door hidden behind the trelliswork, but Bohmer told them to go to the left, where there stood a worn but sturdy oak door.

With footsteps echoing coldly on stone flags, they did as instructed. When they reached the door, Holmes took hold of the ring that served as a handle, twisted it and pushed the portal wide. The door swung inwards with the softest protest of dry hinges.

As he had expected, the stone-walled room beyond had been decked out as a makeshift laboratory. Benches set around the edge of the room held a bewildering assortment of Petri dishes and test tubes, knife switches and bell jars. Beakers filled with gaudily coloured liquids danced and bubbled over Bunsen burners, and jagged lines of electricity climbed the tube of a buzzing Jacob's Ladder. And there, on the far side of the room, stood the stolen influence machine, its two discs whirring in opposite directions as it built up and stored an electrical charge that could kill . . . or just perhaps instil the spark of life.

'Inside,' said Bohmer, and this time he

prodded Watson in the back with the barrel of the blunderbuss to get them both moving. They went deeper into the makeshift laboratory.

The giant was stretched out on a crude operating table in the centre of the flagstone floor, his massive chest rising and falling sluggishly. His shirt had been opened, and the wound in his chest — the bullet wound Watson had inflicted upon him the night before — had been prepared for surgery.

Holmes looked at the person preparing to operate. The sudden stiffening of shoulders beneath a stained white lab coat told him that their entrance had been heard above the bubble and buzz of so much equipment. And when that person turned, he saw the glint of a pistol in the right hand.

'I thought we would find you here,' Holmes said at last. 'But I confess, Fräulein Hertz, I did not expect you to be armed.'

Caroline smiled coolly. 'Well, I wanted to be prepared. After all, it was only a matter of time before you came.'

'And you knew I *would* come,' he said. 'You arranged it that way, didn't you?'

She raised an eyebrow. 'Did I?'

'It was not a difficult mystery to solve; but then it wasn't meant to be, was it?' he replied. 'In the first place, the body of Mauritz Färber was hidden so clumsily that it was quite obviously meant to be found. That in its turn created a crime that required discretion to solve, if the name of Frankenstein were to be protected. Hence the letter that brought me here in the first place.'

'What about it?' she asked.

'In it, the burgomaster implied that he was making the request for my assistance with the full consent of the baron. But when we first met the baron, it was quite clear that our presence here was the very last thing he desired. So someone else must have persuaded the burgomaster to send that letter.' His gimlet eyes bore into hers. 'He is very fond of you, isn't he?'

'He would like to be.'

'And knowing that, you used his loyalty to the baron, and his devotion to you, to persuade him to write that letter.'

'You are every bit as brilliant as I hoped you would be,' she said.

'There is nothing especially brilliant in the process of elimination,' Holmes replied. 'That someone was attempting to follow in Victor Frankenstein's footsteps was obvious. But why should a Frankenstein, with all the money and privilege that goes with such a name, have to steal chemicals and equipment? Only someone with limited funds, and a name that would carry no weight if used to obtain credit, could be behind that. Thus I was able to eliminate the baron and his sons from my enquiry.'

'And that alone convinced you that I was behind it all?'

'By no means. But you have systematically lured me here every step of the way, Fräulein Hertz. I can only wonder why.'

She used the gun to gesture to the body on the table. 'So I could introduce you to him.'

'And he is . . . ?'

'My great-grandfather, Victor von Frankenstein.'

Watson drew a breath. 'So you *are*

Mary Shelley's granddaughter?'

'You worked that out, too?' she asked, clearly impressed. 'Yes, Mary Shelley died giving birth to a child. My mother.'

'A fact known to very few,' Holmes said.

'Of course. And for one very good reason, gentlemen. Because death in childbirth is the *real* curse of Frankenstein! My mother was also its victim. But she continued Mary's work. Using the novel *Frankenstein*, she researched the generation of life with my father. Together, they collected the brain of Victor Frankenstein and preserved it in formalin.'

'And you carried on with their experiments until you succeeded,' breathed Watson.

'My father trained me well. One month ago, I finally animated a body containing my ancestor's brain.'

'And you created a killer,' Watson said.

'He cannot be blamed for his actions. His cells are decaying, and he is slowly losing his identity. I must constantly remind him of who he is.'

'Gangrene has also set in,' noted Holmes.

'How did you know that?'

'That sickly-sweet smell, reminiscent in turns of whiskey and rotting citrus fruits, is quite unmistakable.'

'Very astute, Herr Holmes. Yes, one of Victor's legs became gangrenous, and he took it upon himself to visit the grave-digger, Färber, without telling me. He asked Färber to unearth a new body for him so that we might replace it, but Färber told him we had taken the last decent body in the cemetery and there was nothing else left.'

'But there was Färber himself,' said Holmes. 'An exceptionally tall man whose leg could, if transplanted successfully, make a near-perfect replacement.'

'It was unfortunate that Victor took it upon himself to kill Färber, but he was not to know that Färber was such a lowly specimen; he suffered from a severe nutritional deficiency, which had dam-aged the nerves in his legs and rendered him quite unsuitable for the intended transplant. I didn't even realize it myself until I operated upon him. But I decided to turn the situation to my advantage.'

'To lure me here.'

'Victor's behaviour was becoming increasingly erratic,' she explained. 'I had to find a way to control him.'

'So you somehow fused his brain with that of your dog, Boris, whose loyalty to you was so strong.'

Watson made a soft gagging noise, but Caroline only smiled and shifted her pistol from one hand to the other. 'It was the only solution. I drugged Victor — for I knew he would never willingly agree to such a procedure — and then anaesthetized him and added Boris's brain, connecting it in parallel to the central brain, so that he would react to my orders, or my whistle.'

Watson started. 'That was the whistling sound I heard last night!' he breathed. 'At the time I thought it was just an aberration caused by the blow I received from . . . Victor, there.'

'It was a difficult operation, and the results are crude and not at all aesthetic — but it worked.'

'No,' Holmes said. 'All you did was turn Victor into a slave.'

'A controllable being,' she corrected

him, 'with enormous power, who would prove invaluable to my work — first in demonstrating that my experiments could succeed, and secondly as an assistant alongside Bohmer.'

'Even so, Victor escaped last evening,' Holmes persisted. 'He must have, for you had no earthly reason to give him his freedom, and thus risk discovery.'

'Yes, he escaped. He got out, and found that woman.'

'Christina,' Watson said brokenly.

'Yes, her. And he responded . . . as you might expect a man who has been starved of female companionship to respond.'

'And the baron?' demanded Holmes. 'What became of him?'

For the first time, her face showed genuine regret. 'Last night, the baron — a dear and wonderful man whom I have always idolized — confessed to us that he has been suffering for some time with a malignant growth in his stomach. Although he had consulted the best surgeons in Heidelberg, he was assured that the growth was inoperable and that he could measure the time left to him in months, if not weeks. I couldn't bear to watch him suffer; not when I know that someday very soon I'll be able to give him a strong new body to inhabit.'

She crossed the flagstones to a curtained alcove they hadn't noticed before. Drawing back the curtain, she revealed a shelf upon which sat a row of jars. Holmes sucked in a breath, and with a jolt of pure horror, Watson realized that each one contained a head, neatly severed from its shoulders, floating gently in a thick tinted solution. He had no trouble in recognizing one of them as belonging to the baron.

'I have preserved all these heads and brains in a combination of formaldehyde, glutaraldehyde, ethanol and various humectants,' Caroline said with obvious pride. 'They will remain perfectly safe and untouched by the ravages of time, until I can transplant the brains into healthy bodies.'

'Bodies like that of Victor?' Holmes asked sceptically.

'Victor's patched-up body is but a simple first draft,' she said. 'A preliminary stage! But with his assistance, and the research of my parents, and yes, even the basic findings of Dippel, I am now close to developing an artificial womb; an outside uterus in which I'll be able to grow whole new bodies. No more pain, no more uncertainty — I will control every step of creation. And in these flawless bodies, I shall put the brains of those who left us too early — including those of my mother and father.'

'It's impossible,' Holmes said.

'No, Herr Holmes, it is the future! How much longer do you think women will breed in pain and anguish? I was born from three generations of women who died giving birth. I don't want that to be my legacy as well. I will not suffer the curse of Frankenstein.'

'Your children will be nothing more than the worn ghosts of people who have already lived their allotted time,' he pointed out. 'Their 'perfect' bodies will be a constant reminder of their inhumanity.'

'Nonsense! They will be exactly the same people they were before! You simply refuse to see it as the progress it is — and in that, you disappoint me.'

'I disappoint myself,' Holmes replied grimly. 'For I clearly underestimated the true extent of your madness.'

'Insult me all you will,' she said. 'But you will see things from a more enlightened perspective when I merge your brain with those of my ancestor and my dog.'

Holmes, seeing the absolute insanity in her, felt his jaw muscles work.

'It was always my intention to give Victor an ordered mind; a keen sense of observation and analysis,' she explained. 'With the addition of your brain, Herr Holmes, I see no reason why he should not recover his full faculties, maybe even see them increased! Of course, to support the weight of a skull with three brains, I will need to construct some sort of neck brace, but that should be easy enough.'

He shook his head. 'It is over, Fräulein,' he said softly.

'Oh, no,' was her response. 'The only thing that is over is this conversation. The next step will go somewhat more easily if you cooperate.' She moved to one of the benches, and from a kidney dish took up a syringe filled with dark yellow liquid.

'Holmes . . . ' Watson breathed, throwing a desperate look in Bohmer's direction.

'No need for alarm,' said Caroline. 'But then, I know you have no fear of needles, Herr Holmes.'

Holmes, however, had heard enough. Without warning, he flung himself at her.

15

Kill Them All!

Startled though she was by the movement, Caroline's reactions were lightning-quick. Stepping back out of Holmes's reach, she brought the gun up and fired. The laboratory exploded with sound, and Holmes felt a white-hot lance of pain drill through his left arm. Under its hammer-blow force, he could only stagger backwards, then fall to his knees.

Watson, meanwhile, used the momentary distraction to hurl himself at Bohmer, closing one hand around the barrel of the blunderbuss and forcing it sideways in order to close the distance still further and punch the manservant in the face. Instinctively, Bohmer's finger tightened on the weapon's trigger. Flame and thunder exploded from the flared muzzle to spray in a wide pattern that struck the jars on their shelves. The laboratory was immediately filled with the shattering of glass, the liquid stench of spilled chemicals, and Caroline's screams of rage.

Bohmer yanked the blunderbuss from Watson's grip; but now that it was empty, he could only use it as a club. With a roar he swung it at Watson's head. Watson ducked beneath it, came back up as it whistled past, and buried his fist wrist-deep in the manservant's stomach. Bohmer folded in half with a great, painful exhalation, and Watson took advantage of the distraction to tear the Webley from the man's waistband.

Bohmer swore, began to lift his head, and bunched his fists to fight back. But Watson, his mind still filled with thoughts of Christina and the awful fate she had endured, was in no mood to prolong the encounter. A savage uppercut straightened Bohmer back to his full height, and a right cross that caught the man neatly to the jaw finished him. Bohmer tumbled sideways, stumbled against the table upon with the Jacob's Ladder was still sending buzzing arcs of electricity up between its twin wires — and collapsed right on top of it.

A sudden blast of sound coincided with a bluish-white flare of light, and Bohmer jolted and shook as a searing force in excess of six hundred volts ripped through his skin, muscles and hair. His grisly death seemed to last forever, as did the twitching, shuddering dance that accompanied it. Then a starburst of sparks blew outward from the crude circuit board on the wall above the table, and the power finally cut out. Bohmer, smoke curling from more than a dozen different spots on his body, eyes melted and pouring from their sockets like jellified tears, collapsed and lay still.

Tearing his eyes from the sight, Watson brought the Webley up and yelled, 'Caroline!'

'John — ' she began.

'Don't move!' he snapped. 'You have played your last game with me, Fräulein Hertz.'

Knowing as much, her expression became one of desperation and pure, animal cunning. 'I wasn't playing games with you!' she protested tearfully. 'My feelings are — '

'Your feelings are not even human!' he

cut in. 'You . . . you need help, woman! You are hopelessly, hopelessly — '

'Watson . . . ' Holmes croaked faintly.

Without looking around, Watson said, 'Save your strength, Holmes. I hardly need to hear you expound upon the duplicity of women just now.'

'No,' Holmes managed. 'Behind you . . . '

The shot and the raised voices had woken the creature — Victor — from his morphine-induced sedation. Now the giant chest rose and fell faster with each massive inhalation, and the fingers of one enormous hand flexed and grabbed at the edge of the operating table. Even as they watched, the giant sat up and turned himself laboriously until his long legs, one of them fairly suppurating with gangrene, dangled over the edge. Then he stood up.

In the confines of the laboratory, he looked even bigger than he actually was. The long, angular face he turned toward Holmes was a mottled caricature of humanity, fish-belly white in places, bruised purple in others, with a tracery of red hairline scars running in all directions. The midnight-black hair protruding from beneath the heavy, lopsided bandage was fine and long; the mouth a gash in which sat rows of crooked yellow teeth. The eyes were green and quite amazingly sharp, and they mirrored to perfection the workings of Victor's disordered mind as he took in the scene before him and tried to make sense of it. Finally his eyes snagged on Watson, and the lips peeled back in a snarl.

Perhaps he remembered Watson as the man who had shot him the night before. Perhaps he recognized the gun as a weapon he needed to neutralize. Either way, the snarl became a growl of pure fury; and as Victor hurled himself forward, Caroline screamed, 'Kill them all!'

Once again Holmes threw himself at her. Ignoring the pain in his arm, he grabbed her wrist and shoved it toward the low ceiling even as she depressed the pistol's trigger. The gun fired, and a bullet struck the ceiling and careened off with a hornet's whine, shattering test tubes and Petri dishes on the other side of the room.

Caroline fought back, pummelling Holmes with blows that would have been largely ineffective had not one of them struck the wound in his shoulder. The impact sent pain searing through him; and bending double with eyes screwed shut, he stumbled away from her. When those grey eyes opened again, he saw Watson attempt to intercept Caroline and Caroline strike at him with the butt of her pistol, then vanish through the laboratory door.

Victor, meanwhile, was still pacing slowly, deliberately, toward Watson. Shaking his head to clear it, Watson backed away from him and brought his gun up even though he knew just how ineffective his bullets were likely to be. Throwing a glance at Holmes, he yelled, 'Go after her!'

It was the last thing Holmes wanted to do just then, but do it he must. He staggered past Victor, who closed rapidly on Watson and, grasping him in a bear hug, yanked him off the floor. Watson's face contorted with agony. He kicked his feet against Victor's shins, but to no avail. As the stench of gangrene filled his nostrils and clogged his throat, he felt his ribs being compressed ever tighter, and the world around him beginning to grow dimmer. He felt sure he would hear his ribs splinter any second.

But he wouldn't submit meekly to the seemingly inevitable. As sweat broke out across his forehead and trickled into his eyes, he slowly, slowly brought his right hand up and tilted his wrist so that the Webley was pointed at the soft stitch-marked flesh just beneath Victor's chin. Victor gripped him harder, and he felt the darkness closing in on him again. Watson's protesting kicks grew weaker; the angle of the gun tipped and dropped. Then, summoning whatever reserves he had left, he stuck the barrel of the Webley back under Victor's jaw and pulled the trigger.

Victor jolted as the top of his misshapen head exploded outwards. He staggered a little, but showed no sign of loosening his hold on Watson. Somewhere in the recesses of his mind Watson thought despairingly, *I was wrong. I thought if I could destroy the brain I could destroy the monster.*

Then he remembered that Victor now

had *two* brains. Desperately he shifted aim, fired again, and this time — God help him, he would never forget the sound — Victor's mouth wrenched wide and he howled as Boris's brain burst out through the side of the ruined skull.

Those massive arms finally loosened. Watson fell away from them, his grip on the Webley gone, his legs collapsing beneath him, and all at once he found himself on the floor beside the smouldering remains of Bohmer. Even as he watched, Victor stumbled back into the buckshot-riddled shelf upon which Caroline had stored the heads. Lifeless now, the giant's body collapsed, the shelf came loose, and what remained of the jars crashed to the flagstones, shattering to shards and splashing the fluids they still contained everywhere, while the preserved heads rolled to a halt on the floor.

★ ★ ★

Holmes threw himself out into the secret corridor just as Caroline turned and fired another shot. The muzzle flash split the semi-darkness; chips of stone flew from the wall to Holmes's right and he ducked to avoid them. Then Caroline ducked into the library, and Holmes was once again in pursuit of her.

He burst into the library just as Caroline vanished through the door leading to the lobby beyond. A wave of nausea assailed him, but still he went after her. As he reached the doorway he saw a footman, alerted by the sounds of gunfire and destruction, trying to intercept her.

'What is it, miss? What's — '

In a blind rage now, she fired at him from a distance of no more than twelve inches. Struck in the stomach, the footman clutched his midriff and corkscrewed to the tile floor, where his legs kicked convulsively.

'Caroline!' Holmes cried.

Again she turned in a swirl of skirts, her face a mask of pure insanity now. Even as she fired another shot, Holmes sought cover behind a suit of armour. 'You've ruined everything!' she screamed. 'Not just for me — for the entire world!'

It seemed to Holmes that she reached a

decision then — that there was no future in her experiments, for there was little if anything remaining of them; and no point in running, for there was nowhere she could possibly run to. That being the case, she would finish this business right where she stood.

'And for that,' Caroline hissed venomously, 'you will pay, Herr Holmes.'

She came striding back across the lobby toward him, the pistol extended to arm's length before her, and her finger worked again and again as she emptied it at him.

Holmes did the only thing he could. Putting his good shoulder to the suit of armour, he pushed it ahead of him, using it as cover as he went to meet her for their final confrontation.

Bullets struck the armour, dented it, then bounced off it to career and whine wildly around the lobby. Then, with a suddenness that was shocking, the fusillade ended, to be replaced by a silence that was close to absolute.

For a moment longer Holmes stood behind the bullet-pocked suit of armour, breathing hard, clamping his teeth against the pain in his arm. Then at last he chanced a glance around it.

Caroline lay on her back, her black dress and her white lab coat fanned out around her. Her arms were flung outward. She still held the pistol in her right hand. There was a neat and almost bloodless bullet hole in the centre of her forehead, almost directly above the space between her fine eyebrows.

Shaken to the core, Holmes turned and looked around the lobby. It was empty but for the body of the footman. As he stumbled out from behind the suit of armour, he looked again at Caroline and realized what had happened. One of the shots she had fired at him had ricocheted off the armour's breastplate and flown back toward its source. In effect, she had killed herself.

Holmes sagged, feeling light-headed. The creak of a floorboard made him turn just as Watson limped wearily from the library. He stopped in the doorway, looked from Holmes to Caroline, then back to Holmes.

'Are you . . . ?'

'I'll live,' Holmes assured him, his voice husky with pain.

Watson went to him and examined his arm briefly. Then, working mechanically, he took out a handkerchief and quickly fashioned a tourniquet. As he did so, members of staff began to file into the lobby from the servants' quarters in uncertain silence.

'You, there,' said Watson, addressing another of the footmen. 'Go and find your masters and bring them back here at once. And you,' he said to another, 'get yourself a horse and ride down to Darmstadt. Tell Burgomaster Helder and Oberwachtmeister Reiniger we need them here immediately.' To a third, 'And you — make sure the downstairs library door is shut and locked. No one is to go in there until the burgomaster arrives.' For a moment the staff just stared at him. 'Move!' he barked.

The men he had indicated finally snapped out of their stupor and went to do as instructed. Satisfied with that, Watson looked at one of the maids. 'I fear we are too late to do anything for the footman there. Please fetch blankets with which to cover him and . . . and Fräulein Hertz. Oh — and we'll need hot water and bandages for Herr Holmes.'

'Yes, sir,' said the maid, hurrying away.

Watson squeezed Holmes's good shoulder. 'We'll soon have you patched up, old man,' he said, forcing a reassuring smile. 'And then . . . '

'Then?' Holmes prompted weakly as he allowed Watson to guide him toward the day room.

'Then,' said Watson, feeling hopelessly subdued by the events of the last few minutes, and trying to fend off a wave of absolute despair that threatened to overwhelm him, 'I have to decide how best to tell this story,' he continued. 'It's certain they'll never believe it at *The Strand*.'

'My friend,' Holmes replied softly, 'I fear they will never believe this story anywhere.'

We do hope that you have enjoyed reading this large print book.

Did you know that all of our titles are available for purchase?

We publish a wide range of high quality large print books including:
Romances, Mysteries, Classics
General Fiction
Non Fiction and Westerns

Special interest titles available in large print are:
The Little Oxford Dictionary
Music Book, Song Book
Hymn Book, Service Book

Also available from us courtesy of Oxford University Press:
Young Readers' Dictionary
(large print edition)
Young Readers' Thesaurus
(large print edition)

For further information or a free brochure, please contact us at:
Ulverscroft Large Print Books Ltd.,
The Green, Bradgate Road, Anstey,
Leicester, LE7 7FU, England.
Tel: (00 44) **0116 236 4325**
Fax: (00 44) **0116 234 0205**

GIVE THE GIRL A GUN

Richard Deming

Manville Moon is a private investigator. On a night out with his girlfriend Fausta Moreni, the lovely owner of the El Patio Café, a group of customers invites them both to a private party at an inventor's home, to celebrate the launch of a business venture based on his new device. But soon after their arrival, the inventor is shot dead by an unseen assailant. Police suspicion quickly falls on the boyfriend of one of the guests, and Moon is hired to prove his innocence — plunging him and Fausta into deadly danger . . .